# SPELL STRUCK

## MERRY MAGIC BOOK 1

### SHELLEY RUSSELL NOLAN

## CHAPTER 1

Merry held her breath as she pushed open the door to the solicitor's office with one hand, the other clutching the letter that had brought her here. The letter stated she was a beneficiary to her grandmother's estate.

A grandmother she hadn't known existed until today.

She grimaced at the memory of the scene with her parents after she'd gone over to their house to show them the letter the day before. Her father insisted his mother had been crazy and Merry should "accept nothing from that woman." Her mother lamented naming their only child after a woman who had abandoned her family.

It had taken a bit to calm them down to get the full story. Even then Merry wasn't sure she had it straight. Her grandmother had disappeared when her dad was a child and had been presumed dead, and his father had died three years later, leading him to become a ward of the state. Then, when Merry was five, his mother had turned up and claimed she had been trapped on another world, had used magic to return, and now wanted to be part of the family again. Her father was shocked to find out she had been alive all along, and furious about the ridiculous excuse she'd offered. He'd forbidden her to have any contact with him or Merry and kicked her out of the house, never to be seen or heard from again.

Until now.

Merry didn't blame him for being mad, and it helped her to understand why he had never let her read what he called "airy fairy" books when she was growing up and why he'd declared any movie or television show that featured magic to be off limits. She didn't like going against her parents' wishes, but she was in desperate need of money. She'd lost her job two weeks ago, and a day after that the flat she'd rented for the last year had been sold. Thanks to an error with the original paperwork, the new owners did not have to honour the rental agreement and had given Merry until the end of the month to move out. If whatever her grandmother had left her meant she didn't have to move back in with her parents and kept her going until she found another job, the ensuing drama would be worth it.

Inside the air-conditioned foyer of the solicitor's office, she stood in front of a gleaming black and silver reception desk, smiling nervously at the immaculately groomed woman standing on the other side.

'Ah, hello, I'm Merry Meadows. I mean, Meredith Meadows. I'm here to see Mrs O'Neil.'

The perfectly made up receptionist lifted her nose as she looked Merry up and down, pursing her lips when her gaze took in the long purple hair. From her disapproving expression, the receptionist would agree with Merry's parents about it not being an appropriate colour. Her decision to have her pale blonde hair dyed to help raise money for cancer research had gone down almost as well as the arrival of the solicitor's letter.

'Take a seat, please, Miss Meadows. I'll let Mrs O'Neil know you have arrived.' The receptionist turned around, her heels not making a sound on the plush carpeted floor as she headed to a door set in the wall behind the reception desk.

Merry perched on the edge of a red velvet lounge that was even more plush than the dark grey carpet. She hadn't anticipated needing to dress up for a simple appointment, but her black shorts and shirt and her favourite pair of ankle boots were out of place in her current surroundings.

The lounge was edged with gold trim, while gold scatter cushions were artfully arranged, making her hesitate to get comfortable. She eyed the rest of the furnishings in the reception area, taking in the fresh bouquet of flowers on the main desk and the thick stack of current upmarket magazines on the coffee table in front of the lounge. Everything was opulent and clearly expensive. They even had an enormous chandelier, with hundreds of teardrop shaped crystals, to light the foyer. She couldn't begin to guess how much it cost to have Mrs O'Neil as her solicitor, but it had to be a lot. Had her grandmother been rich?

She shouldn't be thinking this way after just finding out her grandmother had recently died, but if she were to inherit a small fortune it would mean all her problems were solved. Besides, it wasn't as though she had even known her grandmother existed until the day before.

She heard the swish of a door opening and looked up to see the receptionist pointing in her direction. At her side was a motherly looking woman with her hair in a messy bun and wearing a dress in a purple two shades brighter than Merry's hair.

The woman wore a huge smile as she approached and stretched out a hand covered in gaudy rings studded with diamonds, emeralds, sapphires and rubies. 'Oh, my dear, it is so good to meet you at last. Your grandmother spoke about you so often it almost felt as if you were one of my own grandchildren.' She clasped Merry's hand between both of hers and didn't seem inclined to let go. 'You look so much like her. You have the same striking blue eyes. It's as if a young Meredith has come to visit me.'

'Ah...' Merry looked to the sleek receptionist, seeking inspiration. All she got was a raised eyebrow before the receptionist moved to take her place back behind the desk.

Merry pulled her hand free and stood up. 'You knew my grandmother well?'

'Oh yes,' said Mrs O'Neil, still beaming a wide smile. 'We were wonderful friends.'

'Hmm, great,' said Merry, not sure how good of friends they could be if the solicitor wasn't aware that she hadn't even known her grandmother existed before today.

She didn't want to be pushy, but the way the woman kept smiling at her made her want to get out of there as soon as possible. 'Your letter said something about me being a beneficiary of her estate.'

'Yes, of course.' The smile dimmed slightly, and then returned even wider than before. 'Why don't we go to my office and we can go over the details of exactly what you have inherited.'

Merry followed Mrs O'Neil to an office that was even more opulently fitted out than the reception, the bright purple of the solicitor's dress clashing with the red, black and silver decor. Once the door closed behind them, Mrs O'Neil urged Merry to take a seat in front of a steel and smoked glass desk.

'Now, before we discuss your inheritance, I will need to see some identification, to make sure I am dealing with the right person,' said Mrs O'Neil, eyes fixed on Merry. 'I do love your hair, by the way. Purple is my favourite colour. Your grandmother's favourite too; one of the many things she and I had in common.'

Merry managed a slight smile. 'Thank you,' she said, the solicitor's overly friendly manner setting her teeth on edge as she rummaged in her shoulder bag.

The letter had detailed the need for identification, so she had brought her birth certificate, driver's licence and passport. Mrs O'Neil scrutinised all three and jotted down the numbers in neat handwriting on a sheet of paper, and then pulled a manila folder out of a red metal filing cabinet that sat behind her desk. She placed the folder on the desk and Merry saw a white sticker on the front with her name written on it in black pen. Or was that her grandmother's name?

Mrs O'Neil opened the folder, pulled out a white envelope and handed it to Merry.

'Your grandmother requested I give this to you, once you were notified of her death. It contains the deed to her bookshop, *Merry Magic*, as well as the key. As per her instructions, no one has set foot on the premises since she passed so all her belongings are still there. As the sole beneficiary of Meredith's estate, everything she possessed now belongs to you to do with as you wish. The bookshop is located in the locality of Belwich, and there is a small residence above the shop where your dear grandmother resided prior to her death.'

Merry's eyes widened as she clutched the envelope. 'Is that where she died? At her bookshop?' She couldn't imagine having someone die on the premises would be good for future business.

Mrs O'Neil gave a sad sigh, though her wide smile never wavered. 'Your grandmother spent her last days in Belwich Hospital. She did not die at her home. Your home now, if you so choose.'

Merry shook her head. Belwich was a tiny town, probably too small to be even classed as a town, two hours south of Werranton. While her inheritance might offer her a place to live, the job prospects there would be even worse. But maybe the bookshop was making enough money that it would be worth her while to move to Belwich?

Before she could figure out a tactful way to broach the subject, Mrs O'Neil said, 'I'm afraid your grandmother's shop was not doing as well as it could, before she had to close it due to her sudden illness, and what savings she had were used to cover her medical expenses and for her funeral. Even if you were to find someone who wanted to buy her clothes and everything she owned, it would not be enough to keep the shop running for more than a week or two.'

Merry hid her disappointment as she digested the words. 'She's already been buried?' She'd have thought they would have had to notify her father prior to burial at least. He was her next of kin, and he hadn't seemed to be aware of her death when she'd shown him the solicitor's letter.

'According to your grandmother's wishes, you were

not to be contacted until after her funeral. She did not hold with what she viewed as exacerbating the grief of those left behind. She wanted no fuss, and to merely take her final resting place in the town she loved best.'

Mrs O'Neil clapped her hands, making Merry jump. 'Now, I am sure this is a lot to take in, but there is one other matter I need to discuss with you. One I believe you will be very interested in.' She reached back into the manila folder and pulled out several sheets of paper stapled together.

'Soon after your grandmother passed away, I was contacted by a client who wishes to purchase the book-shop. They have made a very generous offer and I really think you should consider it.' Mrs O'Neil gave an indulgent smile. 'A young lady like yourself would not wish to be stuck in such a small town as Belwich or running a shop that is unable to even cover the oper-ating costs.'

Merry frowned. While the idea of being stuck in a small town did suck, she didn't like the patronising way Mrs O'Neil was looking at her. 'If it's not making any money, why does your client want to buy it?'

Mrs O'Neil's lips firmed in a line. 'I believe their intent is to repurpose the space in a more fitting manner than a bookshop. They have made numerous offers to your grandmother over the years, but she refused to sell, even though it was clear her mental faculties were, shall we say, not at their best. They are hoping you're more willing to see reason than she was.' She circled a section of the first piece of paper in red pen and then shoved it over to Merry.

Merry looked down, eyes focusing on the amount that was circled. She gasped.

$125,000.

That would more than see her through until she could find a new job. No more worrying about being able to pay the rent on a new flat or waiting to qualify for unemployment benefits. She'd be free to start over, without debts.

She looked up at Mrs O'Neil, who wore a smug expression as she held out a black pen. 'Just sign and date on the pages I have marked for you and I will take care of everything. I promise, you will never receive a better offer.'

Merry's eyes skimmed over the first page of the paperwork, not understanding half of what she was reading, except that it was a contract for the sale of *Merry Magic.*

The name tugged at her.

Her nickname. Maybe even the same nickname her grandmother had been known by.

'Once you sign, all your financial troubles will be over, my dear.'

Merry frowned at the eagerness in Mrs O'Neil's voice. She put the pen down. 'Do you mind if I take some time to think about it?' At the very least she needed to read over the contract, preferably with a legal dictionary handy. There were so many clauses and big words on the first page that Merry could be signing anything. This was all happening so fast. She needed to stop and think about it.

'What's there to think about? You need money, and my clients are willing to pay handsomely.'

Merry stiffened. 'How do you know I need money?'

Mrs O'Neil gave a start and then covered with a little laugh. 'You're nineteen years old. All teenage girls need money.'

Merry stood, stuffing the contract and the envelope with the deed and key to *Merry Magic* into her bag. 'I would like to take some time to consider this offer before I make up my mind.'

Mrs O'Neil stood and gave Merry a smile that looked forced. 'Don't consider it too long. The offer is only valid to the end of the month. The utilities have also been paid up until then. After that, you're on your own.' For the first time, the tone of her voice was hard, almost threatening. The stare the solicitor gave her was just as hard as her tone.

Merry ducked her head and exited the office, clutching her bag tightly as she wondered if her crazy grandmother's inheritance was going to prove to be more trouble than it was worth.

During the drive home, she puzzled over the strange encounter with Mrs O'Neil. The way the solicitor had looked at her, as she'd left without signing the contract, had been chilling. A far cry from all the gushing and smiling and talk of how wonderful friends she and

Merry's grandmother had been. Her manner had been very off-putting as had been the pressure to sign the contract there and then. As if anyone, on learning they had just inherited a business, would sign it away without first checking if the offer was a good one or not.

When she reached the flat, she let herself in, made her way to the kitchen and placed her bag on the dining table. She reached inside and pulled out the envelope containing the deed and key to *Merry Magic*. She opened it up, only to find they were not the only things inside.

Written in a shaky hand, on pale purple paper, was a letter addressed to her.

*To my darling Merry,*

*I CAN NEVER TELL you how sorry I am that we never got to meet in person. I have watched over you through the years and you have always been in my thoughts. Please don't be mad at your father for keeping us apart. He had his reasons, as did I in respecting his wishes to stop trying to contact you until now, when it is far too late for us to have the relationship I have long dreamed of.*

*I can never make up for missing out on being a part of your life, but know that I have always loved you, and I named my shop for you. While we may share the same first name, no one has ever called me Merry. I hope Merry Magic brings you as much happiness as it did me, and that it makes up in some small way for my absence in your life.*

*Until we meet again in the next life, may the magic of the world shine upon you.*

*Love always,*
*Meredith*

Merry wiped a tear away as she reread the letter, wishing she had been given the chance to know her grandmother. It was hard not to feel anger at her parents, her father especially, for keeping them apart. Then again, if her mother suddenly disappeared only to turn up years later talking about magic and other worlds maybe she would feel the same.

Either way, there was no way of knowing how she and her grandmother may have got on.

Had her grandmother really been crazy?

The letter didn't read that way, and she'd named her bookshop after Merry.

Merry pulled the contract out of her bag and placed it on the dining table. $125,000 was a lot of money. An offer too good to be passed up, Mrs O'Neil had said. Maybe.

Merry had no idea what the market price was for bookshops, especially one that wasn't making any money. For all she knew, the place could be worth twice as much and Mrs O'Neil's claim it was going broke might be a lie so she could earn herself a fat commission by brokering the sale. No way was she going to trust a solicitor she had only just met. She had no idea who it was that wanted to buy the bookshop, or if Mrs O'Neil was right in saying it was the best offer she would ever get.

It was time to see if the solicitor had been telling the truth.

She scooped up her bag and the paperwork, headed to her room and switched on her laptop. While she waited for the laptop to boot up, she read over the contract, trying to make sense of the legal jargon. On the last page, she saw the name of a corporation listed under the line marked as buyer.

*Huntington Inc.*

Merry frowned. The name sounded familiar. Where had she heard it before?

She typed the name into the search engine and scrolled through the first page of hits, but nothing jumped out at her. She clicked the link titled "News" and one article came up, listing a recent purchase by *Huntington Inc.* of a commercial property. She scrolled down until she found the address, gasping when she recognised it.

207 Quay Lane.

The same address as the shopping centre that housed *Bling and Baubles*, the place where Merry had worked since finishing high school, until it was sold and the new owner evicted all the tenants thanks to a legal loophole. *Huntington Inc.* was the reason Merry lost her job, and now they wanted to buy her grandmother's bookshop from her. She scanned the article and a chill swept over her when she saw the date the sale had gone through. The same date her grandmother died.

It couldn't be a coincidence.

Could it?

She looked to see if there was an address listed for *Huntington Inc.* but all that came up was an email address and a phone number. She dialled the number and got an answering machine. She hung up the phone without leaving a message, undecided as to what to do now.

If they were so keen to buy the bookshop that they were willing to go to such lengths as to put her out of work, there had to be a reason. She intended to find it out. She had less than a month to make up her mind as to whether to sell the bookshop. She was going to use that time wisely, starting now.

Merry stuffed the contract and the keys to *Merry Magic* back into her bag. Then she raced to her car and set her phone's GPS for Belwich. With the bland tones of the GPS giving directions, she backed out of the driveway.

Alone with her thoughts, Merry spent the two-hour drive trying to come up with a plausible reason that did not involve some company scheming to buy her inheritance. The closer she got to Belwich, the more she wondered if she was overreacting. She was almost tempted to turn around, but she'd come so far already. Besides, didn't she owe it to her grandmother to at least visit the bookshop that had been named after her?

When she pulled up in what appeared to be the main

street of Belwich, it was late afternoon. There were few cars or people on the streets, but those that were about turned to stare at Merry and her purple hatchback as she drove by. She grimaced, sure they had noted she was an outsider. In a town this small, everyone probably knew each other and what kinds of cars they all drove. She pushed that thought out of her mind as the GPS announced she was nearing her destination.

There, a splash of colour among the other plain shopfronts stood out, and she parked in front of it and got out of the car, letting her eyes take it all in.

A colourful design, shimmering in blues and purples, showed an open book from which magical sparkles danced above the page. It was beautiful, as were the words written above the image of an open book in the centre of the display - *"Merry Magic - Where an adventure awaits on every page."*

Merry hadn't read many physical books since she had finished high school, moved out and been able to sign up for streaming services to binge watch all the television shows and movies her parents had never allowed her to watch. She'd made up for it by listening to audiobooks while she created jewellery to sell in *Bling and Baubles*. That shop was now closed, thanks to *Huntington Inc.*

Merry hunted in her bag for the envelope containing the key as she stepped towards the wooden front door, smiling to see that it had been painted to resemble a magical portal. The care her grandmother had made with the outside of the shop made her eager to see what awaited her inside.

'Excuse me, are you Meredith Meadows?'

Gasping at the question posed in a male's voice, Merry spun around, a hand going to her throat when she spied a strange man standing a short distance away. There had been no one in sight when she got out of her car. Where the hell had he come from?

'Sorry, I didn't mean to startle you.'

Merry shook her head. 'It's fine.' She ventured a smile towards the stranger standing at the kerb in front of her car. He held a briefcase.

The smile died as he stepped closer. Okay, maybe it wasn't fine.

# CHAPTER 2

The guy was tall, with greying brown hair that was shaved almost to the scalp. His skin was so pale it washed him out, and his light blue eyes were rimmed in red. Sweat gleamed on his brow and he used the sleeve of his white shirt to wipe it away when he came to a stop too close for Merry's liking.

From the damp look of his sleeve, he had been sweating copiously for some time.

Was he ill?

Merry took a step back, pressing against the book-shop door as he leaned his head towards her.

'You are Meredith Meadows, the granddaughter of Meredith Meadows?'

'Ah…' Merry scanned the street to see if anyone else was about. This guy gave off a weird vibe, his reddened eyes narrowing as he stared at her, thin colourless lips firming into a line.

'You must be her granddaughter. No one else has come near the place in weeks; certainly none that looked like you.'

Merry stiffened when he looked at her hair, his lip curling in a sneer.

She pushed aside her unease to glare at him. 'Who are you? What do you want?'

He smoothed down his shirt and lifted his chin, all the better to sneer down his nose at her. 'I represent *Huntington Inc.* I understand you have been informed of our offer to purchase this place.' He waved a hand towards the bookshop's window without taking his eyes off Merry.

Seriously? Her unease returned at having him turn up out of the blue. Maybe she wasn't paranoid to think they had caused the closure of *Bling and Baubles* just to put her in a position where she had to sell them the bookshop.

She narrowed her eyes. 'Mrs O'Neil mentioned something about that, yes.'

'Excellent.' He rubbed his palms together and an oily smile settled on his thin lips. 'I am sure, now that you've seen the place, you are ready to sign the contract.' He delved into a pocket of his dark grey trousers and pulled out a pen.

'Do you have the contract here with you?' He leaned closer, an avid look in his eyes. 'I am authorised to sign on the company's behalf. I also have a copy of the contract in my briefcase, if you did not bring yours.' He sniffed. 'This should have all been taken care of in the solicitor's office, but no matter. We can cover the essentials now. All I need to know is if you would prefer a bank cheque or payment direct into your bank account?'

'Whoa, hang on a minute.' Merry held up her hands, palms out, when he tried to hand the pen to her. 'I didn't come here to sign the contract.'

What the hell was wrong with him? No way she was signing anything.

'I'm sure once I have properly explained our offer, you will change your mind.' He gave a condescending smile as he waved the hand holding the pen at the locked door to *Merry Magic* behind her. 'If you invite me inside we can take a seat while we talk this through. You do have the key with you, don't you?'

His eyes narrowed as he waited for her response.

Merry gripped her bag tightly, hugging it to her body. 'Actually, I came here to pay my respects to my grandmother, at her final resting place.' She sidestepped around him. 'So, if you'll excuse me, I need to go and do that.' When she reached her car door, she looked back to find him hovering just behind her.

'I'll wait here until you return, then,' he said.

For the first time, a flare of alarm sizzled through her. How far was *Huntington Inc.* willing to go to get her to sell? No one knew she was here. She'd visited her parents yesterday, and her decision to go against their wishes and see what her inheritance entailed meant they may not try to contact her for a few days.

Merry scanned the street and was relieved to see a woman pushing a pram come out of a shop two doors down from *Merry Magic* and head their way. She did not want to be alone with this guy a moment longer.

She gritted her teeth and attempted a sincere smile. 'There's no need for you to wait for me. I'll be heading home as soon as I leave the cemetery.' When he stepped even closer, she held up a hand. 'I'll contact Mrs O'Neil when I get back to Werranton, to discuss the contract. Until then, I have nothing further to say on the matter.'

Merry shot him a glare, grabbed her keys out of her bag and unlocked her car. Once she was inside, with the door closed, she hit the button to lock all the doors. The guy was giving her the major creeps. She wouldn't put it past him to open the passenger door and climb into the car so he could continue to badger her about signing the contract. She quickly got the car started and reversed out of the park. She drove off down the street, with no idea where she was going, just needing to get away from him.

She had no intention of going to the cemetery; in case he followed her. She just wanted to go home and forget Belwich ever existed.

A pang of guilt went through her at not even making it inside the bookshop. Her grandmother's note had made it clear she had loved the shop and from what Merry had seen, her grandmother had done her best to make it a magical place. She would never get to step inside it if she let *Huntington Inc.* scare her off.

Still, she had until the end of the month, four weeks away, before their offer to buy it expired. Just because she hadn't gone in today didn't mean she could never go inside. Maybe she would be able to get one of her friends to come back with her, a whole carload of them even. That way she wouldn't be alone if Mr Creepy showed up again.

When she turned the next corner, she slowed as she scanned the street and spotted the Belwich Cemetery on her left. This was the place the grandmother she had never met was buried. The place she had just told Mr Creepy that she had intended to go to next. He wouldn't really follow her, would he?

Without conscious thought, she pulled into the tiny carpark and turned off the engine.

Hand still on the keys in the ignition, ready to flee if necessary, she scanned the street behind her. There was no sign of Mr Creepy, or anyone else. She should be fine to quickly jump out and find her grandmother's grave to pay her respects. She'd come all this way. It would be a shame to go home having allowed Mr Creepy to scare her off from the cemetery as well as the bookshop.

The cemetery was quite small, same as the town, so it shouldn't take her long to do what she needed to do and get out of there.

Merry straightened her shoulders and got out of the car, ears pricked for any sign she was no longer alone. She wouldn't let Mr Creepy sneak up on her again.

A chill wind swept through the cemetery, creating

goose bumps on her bare arms and legs. She reached into her bag to grab out a gauzy black wrap and draped it around her shoulders. It wasn't much, but it was better than nothing. She needed to find her grandmother's grave and get out of there.

Lush grass lay underfoot as she moved through the first row of graves. The plots were all tidy, well-tended, many with small ornaments and floral arrangements on them, dates on the tombstones showing these were from the last decade. She scanned among them for her grandmother's name but couldn't find it.

A line of trees separated this section of the cemetery from the rest and she headed that way. The shadows were deeper when she stepped into the tree line and her boots crunched on dried leaves. Merry stopped a moment to get her bearings. The graves on the other side were all much older than those closest to the carpark. The tombstones were weathered, though the plots were as well maintained here as in the newer section. On the off chance her grandmother was among them, having perhaps purchased a plot decades before, she searched down each row. She reached the last of them, still without finding her grandmother's grave.

Had the solicitor been mistaken, or did Belwich have another cemetery?

For a town this size, surely one cemetery would be sufficient?

Merry scanned the cemetery one last time, her eyes following the path that led to a one storey brick chapel.

She set off that way, the chill wind rising and whipping her long hair around her face, but she didn't want to stop to hunt in her bag for a hair tie. The closer she got to the chapel, the darker it seemed to get. Trees lined either side of the path as it wound around the side of the chapel, and soft shuffling noises came from the leaves that had fallen to the ground. At first, she put it down to the wind, but then she caught a flicker of movement out of the corner of her eye.

Something was in the cemetery, keeping pace with her. She stopped and peered into the underbrush but could see nothing. The noise had ceased as soon as she'd stopped walking.

Was it a snake?

The thought of one slithering across the path made her shudder, and not just because Australia had a large number of venomous snakes. Creatures that slithered or crawled gave her nightmares and, despite the shadows, the day was still too bright for whatever had made the noise to be a possum. She hurried down the path, casting quick glances left and right, but the noise was not repeated.

She reached the back of the chapel and saw a section that contained three rows of graves, with empty land beyond them. She stepped up to the first row, scanning the tombstones, the hairs on her arms and the back of her neck rising, sure she could feel the presence of some-one, something, watching her. She stopped walking, looking back at the chapel, unable to see anyone. Yet that sense of being watched never faded. If she had a nightmare tonight, it wouldn't be on account of some creepy crawly. She'd be stuck in a haunted graveyard for sure.

Maybe this hadn't been a good idea. What if Mr Creepy really had followed her? Merry swallowed down a lump in her throat at the thought of being confronted by him in the middle of a deserted cemetery. She should go back to the car, drive home, and sign the bloody contract. Who cared if the solicitor was pushy and the company representative creepy? The money would give Merry her life back.

She tensed, intending to leave, but the flash of movement came again, this time from the other side of her.

She spun around and froze.

A small black cat sat on a tombstone one row back, staring at her with its gleaming yellow eyes. Relief surged through Merry as she realised it was the cat that had made the noises. It must have been what she'd sensed watching her, as well.

'You scared me, little kitty,' she said as she moved towards it, a hand stretched out to touch its shiny coat.

The cat bounded away before she could touch it, winding its way through the last row of tombstones, taking a perch on top of one that had a statue of an iridescent angel reading a book on top. Merry followed the cat, somehow sure of what she would find when she got close enough to read the inscription below the angel.

Sure enough, it was her grandmother's grave, though

a chill swept over her as she read the name, Meredith Meadows.

Her name.

Not that many people other than her parents ever called her Meredith.

She was Merry to her friends. Still, it was weird to see her name on a tombstone. She pushed that feeling aside as she knelt down and gazed upon the grave of a grandmother she had never known existed until the day before.

She gave a sigh. 'I wish I'd had the chance to meet you. It doesn't seem fair that you could have lived only two hours away and I never knew. But you knew. You even named your shop after me.'

Tears pricked Merry's eyes. How hard must it have been for her grandmother to know Merry was so close but to be forbidden to contact her. Was her grandmother really crazy, as her parents had said?

She would never know the answers to these questions. All she had to go on was what she'd been told. Though maybe there was someone here in Belwich who could tell her more about her grandmother. Surely the locals, who had to know everybody in their tiny town, could shed some light on the woman who was buried here?

Something soft brushed against her leg, and she looked down to see the cat rubbing up against her. This time the cat let Merry pat it, the fur silk beneath her fingers. The cat began to purr, butting its head against her hand.

A soft clink came, and Merry saw something shiny dangling from a silver collar around the cat's neck. With slow movements, so she didn't startle the little cat, she used her other hand to slide the collar around so she could see what it was.

A small metal disc, with a name engraved on it gleamed against the black fur.

'Sadie,' said Merry, and the cat stopped purring and gazed up at her. 'That's your name, huh? It's pretty. I like it.'

The cat bounded away a few steps and then stopped to groom herself while Merry got to her feet, conscious of the spreading shadows in the cemetery.

'Well, Sadie, I guess it's time for me to go home.'

The cat didn't even look up from its bath as Merry started walking towards the path that led around the chapel. By the time she reached her car, it was almost six o'clock, and Merry's stomach was rumbling. Lunch had been a long time ago. She should have packed a snack before she left home.

She had no money to buy anything, so it would be two hours before she had a chance to feed her hunger. Although, maybe she didn't have to wait that long. Mrs O'Neil had said no one had entered the bookshop since her grandmother had died, and the residence above it was still filled with all of her grandmother's belongings. Maybe that would mean food too. Food that, along with everything else, now belonged to Merry. Besides, Mr Creepy had to be long gone by now, so there was nothing to stop her checking out the bookshop while she was in town. If she did decide to sell, she would never have to return to Belwich if she visited the bookshop now and figured out what, if any, of her grandmother's things she wanted to keep.

Decision made, she drove back to the main street and once again parked in front of the bookshop. This time, no creepy stranger lurked nearby so she quickly grabbed the key out of the envelope and let herself in, smiling again at the feeling of entering a magical portal inspired by the painted wooden door.

She locked the door behind her, just in case Mr Creepy did turn up again, and then felt on the wall beside the door for a light switch. She found it and turned it on, and then gazed around her in wonder as sparkling fairy lights lit up the interior of the bookshop.

A small counter was set against the wall to the left of the door, while shelves filled the right side of the room. Two small couches in front of the window, just waited for readers to curl up with their selections, while figurines of fantastical creatures shared shelf space with books. Bright paintings of fantasy scenes hung on the walls and there was even a children's reading nook comprising a castle cubby filled with colourful cushions.

As much as it was lovely and inviting, there was no food here to stop the grumbling in her stomach. She would come back down here to explore once she'd had something to eat.

Merry headed towards the back of the bookshop, winding between shelves to a doorway covered with a shimmering purple curtain. She pushed the curtain aside and stepped into a small office space. There was a door on the other side, nestled between a desk and a filing cabinet. This door led to a narrow hall with an equally narrow stairway at the end of it.

The wooden treads of the stairs were worn but clean and a light beckoned at the top. Merry slowly made her way up the stairs and into the place where her grandmother had lived.

A lamp sitting on a side table beside a plush recliner had been left on and it illuminated a small but neat lounge room. A couch that matched those in the bookshop sat against the wall opposite the recliner, with doorways on either side of it. One led to what looked to be a kitchen, so Merry headed in that direction, switching on the lights as she went.

The kitchen was as small as the lounge, with a round table and four chairs nestled in one corner. The appliances were old but clean and Merry moved towards the wall that held a large cupboard and a refrigerator.

One glance in the fridge told her that whatever was in there was out of date, and she quickly closed the door, hand waving away the smell of vegetables left to rot. Then she turned to the pantry, her stomach rumbling in appreciation when she spotted an unopened packet of sweet biscuits.

She grabbed the packet from the shelf and ripped it open, taking out a biscuit and stuffing it in her mouth even as she turned around, intending to see where the other door off the lounge led.

She stopped, biscuit congealing in her mouth, at the sight of a small timber box with a brass lock sitting in the middle of the table. The box was roughly the size of a hardcover book, and it seemed to glow with a soft light.

That hadn't been there before, had it?

Swallowing the remains of her biscuit, Merry moved closer to the table, sure she would have remembered seeing the box when she first entered the kitchen if it had been there. Or had she been so focused on finding food her eyes had skimmed over it?

She'd made it halfway to the table when a streak of black intercepted her, dashing between her feet.

Merry stumbled forward, dropping the biscuit packet as she tried to avoid stepping on the cat from the cemetery, arms flailing as she sought to right her balance. One hand came down on the box on the table, the edge of the brass lock cutting into her palm.

'Ouch!' Merry grabbed the back of a chair and finally managed to steady herself even as a roar, like a rushing wind, came from nearby. She turned around, seeking the source of the noise. And where the hell had the cat come from? Had it followed her from the cemetery and found an open window somewhere to get inside?

A meow came from behind her and she spun back around to find the cat sitting on top of the timber box. She lunged forward, even as the sound of the wind intensified. One hand touched the cat's back as the other grabbed hold of the timber box, the roar of the wind all she could hear.

But now the wind was there in the kitchen, pushing and pulling at her.

Merry cried out as she felt herself being lifted, hair whipping around her face as she was flung into the air. She screamed, sure she was going to slam into the ceiling, but all she met was empty air.

The wind whirled her around, the sound of it drowning out her screams as she was spun over and over. She kept screaming until the breath was ripped from her lungs and blackness swept over her.

$\mathcal{E}$ars ringing, head pounding, Merry forced her eyes to open. She quickly closed them again when what she saw did not make sense. Instead of the ceiling of her grandmother's tiny residence above the bookshop, she had looked up at a cloudless blue sky, large trees helping to shade her from the sun's rays. It should be the moon's turn to shine.

A light weight landed on her chest and something soft poked her chin.

She opened her eyes and found herself staring into the yellow gaze of the little black cat, Sadie. The cat stood on all fours staring intently at Merry.

Merry groaned as the cat sat on its haunches and began to groom itself. She heaved out another groan as she struggled into a sitting position, dislodging the cat in the process. With a squawked meow, the cat leapt aside.

*Was that really necessary?* The voice was tart, filled with indignation.

Merry gasped and looked around, unable to see who had spoken. She scrambled to her feet, heart pounding as she pushed hair off her face.

She swayed when she was upright, dizziness swamping her, and stumbled a few steps to place a hand against one of the trees trunks to steady herself. Tree trunks definitely did not belong in her grandmother's kitchen. Or was she still in the cemetery? Maybe she had encountered someone or something more dangerous than the cat while searching for her grandmother's grave and the trip to the bookshop had been a hallucination brought on by trauma. If she'd been attacked and left unconscious on the ground all night, it would explain why it was now daylight.

*You were not attacked and have only been unconscious a few moments. Your body is merely reacting to your first instance of portal travelling. It can take some getting used to, but the effects will wear off soon, and you will adapt to the different time.*

Portal travelling? Different time zones? What the hell?

Merry scanned the nearby trees. 'Who are you? Where are you?' She still couldn't see anyone, and all she could hear was the soft whisper of wind through the leaves of the tree she was leaning against. A tree that still should not be there.

What the hell was going on?'

*I would have thought it would be obvious. You triggered the spell your grandmother used to transport herself between worlds.* The voice was dry. *As for who I am, I am Sadie, your grandmother's companion.*

Sadie?

The cat?

Merry looked downward to see the cat sitting near her feet, alert gaze fixed on her.

The wave of dizziness from before returned tenfold, taking the strength from Merry's legs. She slid down the tree trunk until she hit the ground, all with the cat, Sadie, watching on. The cat didn't move; didn't blink.

Merry swallowed against a sudden dryness in her mouth as she tried to process what the cat had said.

A hysterical laugh threatened to erupt at that.

The cat had spoken. About portals, spells and other worlds.

'I'm crazy, aren't I?' The question didn't require an answer. Of course she was crazy. Or she hit her head when the freak wind whipped through her grandmother's kitchen. A wind that had appeared out of nowhere. Just like the small timber box that had appeared on the table.

The cat narrowed its eyes, tail flicking from side to side. *We don't have time for this, so I will say it only once. You are not crazy. You are a witch, with the potential to become a mage just like your grandmother, and you have transported us to the world she and I were born in. Tirana.*

Merry slumped down even more, chin down, eyes closed

Her parents had said her grandmother was crazy, talking about magic and other worlds. This must be what it was like. Would her father refuse to have anything to do with Merry, now that she was also crazy? Was craziness inherited? Or maybe the kind of crazy her grandmother had been was contagious. It had to be, for her delusion, hallucination, whatever this was, to deal with the same type of things as what had afflicted her grandmother. Hallucinations had started minutes after she'd set foot in the bookshop.

A sharp pain shot through Merry's wrist and her eyes snapped open in time to see the cat leaning back.

'You bit me. Why would you do that?'

The cat gracefully lifted one paw and licked it, and then placed it down before looking at Merry. *As I said, we don't have time for this. It is my duty to introduce you to your true heritage.*

Merry pushed herself up and stood, glad to see the dizziness had worn off and she no longer felt her legs were going to collapse beneath her at any second. 'I didn't bring us here, wherever here is. It's not even real. It can't be real.'

'Ouch!' Merry glared down at the cat, and then bent down to rub the fresh bite mark on her ankle. 'Stop biting me.'

The cat jumped to its feet, tail swishing from side to side even faster. *Do you think I like biting you? Humans taste dreadful. But I need you to stop your whining and listen to me. We need to get you back to your world before someone sees you. Your grandmother had many enemies who will not be pleased to have one of her bloodline showing up in Tirana.*

A cold shiver swept over Merry as she scanned the trees, waiting for said enemies to jump out. But they were alone. Then she shook her head, half convinced she was dreaming, even if the bites on her wrist and ankle were still stinging.

Maybe it would help her get out of this dream, hallucination, or whatever it was, if she played along. 'Okay, cat, you win. How do we get back to my world?'

The cat glared up at her, eyes narrowed to slits. *My name is Sadie, not cat, and we return the same way we came. We use your grandmother's spell box.*

Spell box? She must mean the timber box. The one that had suddenly appeared on the table in her grandmother's kitchen. She had cut her palm on the brass lock and remembered clutching it and the cat when the wind had lifted her up.

Merry scanned the ground near where she had been laying. 'Where is it?'

The cat's head… Sadie's head, swivelled as she looked around the small clearing. *I don't see it. You must have let go while we were travelling through the portal.* She turned back to fix a hard gaze on Merry. For a cat, her face was very expressive. *Lesson one, a witch must never let go when they trigger a spell box.*

'I'm not a witch. How was I supposed to know?'

Sadie gave a snort. *If you weren't a witch, and one of your grandmother's bloodline at that, the spell would never have been triggered. It was your blood on the chest that brought us here.*

Merry stiffened as she rubbed at the wound in the centre of her palm. It had stopped bleeding, but the sting started up again at the reminder.

*If we're lucky, the spell box will not have landed far away.* Sadie's voice was cool as she poked her nose into the bushes beside one of the trees. *If we're not lucky... well, let's not worry about that until we have to.*

'How is it that you can talk?' Merry asked as she checked behind the tree trunk she had used to steady herself on. A cat's vocal cords were not designed for speech, not human speech anyway, and she hadn't noticed Sadie's mouth open when she spoke.

*A companion is able to project her words directly into the mind of her witch.*

Merry left the statement she was a witch alone for now. 'Why didn't you talk to me before, back in Belwich?' Not that any of this could be real. Magic only existed in books, and so did talking cats.

*Your magical nature was dormant until you touched the spell box. I would have been able to converse with you then, but you transported us here before I could do so.* The tone was cool, with a hint of rebuke. *Now, less talking and more searching. We can discuss the differences between our worlds once we are safely returned to Belwich.*

With a shake of her head at being reprimanded by a

cat, Merry continued her search. After checking in the rest of the bushes scattered among the trees on the other side of the small clearing she turned to Sadie. 'It's not here.'

Mild alarm pushed through her as the cat also reported no success. There was no reason to get all worked up. None of this was real. Couldn't be real. Yet the longer the hallucination lasted the more real it felt. The rough bark of the trees and the way the leaves crinkled as she'd brushed them aside had felt very real. Sure, there were plenty of people who believed they were witches, and Wicca had roots all over the world. But it wasn't possible that touching a timber box could have transported her to another world, one where a cat was capable of talking via telepathy.

The talking cat in question swivelled her head, nose twitching as she did so. *This way.* She bounded through a small gap in the bushes between two trees, sleek body sliding easily through.

Merry hurried after her, bushes catching on her hair as she squeezed past, and followed the little cat as she wound her way between even more trees. These looked nothing like the ones that commonly grew in Central Queensland where she had grown up. Merry was accustomed to seeing trees devoid of leaves, the grass straggly and brown thanks to lack of rain. The trees around them were covered in leaves in various shades of green, while the thick grass underfoot was soft and springy. There was also a crispness to the air, and a silence broken only by the occasional call of a bird. There was no sound or sign of distant traffic or anything else that signalled the presence of civilisation. They could be in the middle of nowhere, for all Merry knew.

To distract herself from the differences in her surroundings, she focused on learning more about the cat. 'You said you were my grandmother's companion. Is that like a familiar?' She knew many stories about witches featured black cats as familiars.

Up ahead, Sadie's lithe body stiffened, though she did not stop. *Familiar is the term used by the guild, but I prefer to think of myself as a companion. A familiar is expected to be subservient, whereas I, as a companion, follow my own path. That path happened to coincide with the path your grandmother was on.*

'Do all witches in Tirana have a black cat as their familiar or companion?'

*Many species of animals are capable of becoming a familiar, though few witches are powerful enough to hear them. Familiars only bond with those who have mastered one or more elements and have gained the status as mages. It is far more difficult for a familiar to become a companion. I do not know of any other cat, black or otherwise, to have attained that distinction.*

Merry stifled a snort. Sadie sounded as if she didn't think any other cat would ever meet her standards. But then, from her experience with non-talking cats, most of them had also been assured of their own importance.

*Oh dear. This is not good.*

Merry pushed through a gap between two bushes that were as tall as she was, and looked ahead to see Sadie standing still, peering down at something. She hurried to join the cat and found herself standing on top of a sloping hill, looking down over a lush valley of rolling green hills. But it was not the view that caught her attention. It was a black-haired woman in a flowing emerald green dress at the base of the hill that caught her eye.

The woman was crouching, the distance making it hard to see what it was she was doing. As Merry watched, the woman stood up, holding something, and strode off in the other direction, away from the hill.

*Hurry. She has the spell box. We must catch her before she makes it to Dryton.* Sadie started down the hill at a fast pace.

Merry, trusting the cat had far better eyesight than her, headed down the hill after Sadie.

The slope was not all that steep, but Merry's leg muscles began to burn before they were halfway down. Sadie appeared to have a much easier time of it, bounding forward and quickly outpacing Merry. By the time she reached the bottom of the hill, Sadie had disappeared in the same direction as the woman who had picked up the spell box.

'Sadie, wait for me.' Panic thrummed through Merry at the thought of getting lost in this strange world. Some of her doubt it was not real, that it was some kind of hallucination, was wearing off. What would she do, if she lost both Sadie and the spell box? How was she supposed to get home then?

This was all so surreal. Her father had cut all contact with her grandmother because he'd believed she was crazy, talking about magic and other worlds. If what Merry was experiencing now was real, her father had been wrong.

Her breath caught.

Her grandmother had disappeared for years. Had she been trapped in Tirana all that time?

How sad to think of how long her grandmother had been estranged from her family, all because no one had believed her. Would they think Merry was crazy too, when she returned and told them what had happened?

That was a problem for another time. First, she had to find Sadie and the spell box.

A rustle came from the bushes to one side of Merry and she gave a sigh of relief when Sadie appeared.

The cat looked Merry up and down. *We have a problem. The girl has headed to Dryton, as I suspected, so we will have to follow her. But you are going to attract attention, dressed like that.*

Merry looked down at her shorts and black t-shirt. She was still wearing her flimsy wrap, too, though it was not as cold here as it had been in the cemetery. The woman they were following had been wearing a flowing dress that covered her from neck to toe, with long sleeves.

Yes, she was going to stand out.

'Is standing out going to be a bad thing?' What were the odds one of her grandmother's enemies, the ones Sadie had mentioned, would spot her? Even if they did, how would they know Merry was her granddaughter?

Sadie snorted. *Your grandmother is well known throughout all of Tirana. You look very much like her, except for your hair colour.*

Hair that was still hanging around her shoulders. Merry reached into her bag and found a hair tie, quickly twisting her hair up into a messy bun and securing it. She didn't have a hat, but she draped the wrap over her head and wrapped it around her neck to partially screen her face. She couldn't do anything about her clothes, so this would have to do.

Then she had a thought. 'Can't you go into Dryton to find the girl and the spell box?'

Sadie twitched. *I am not her companion, and her clothing marked her as a witch, not a mage. She will be unlikely to hear me.*

Merry's mouth dropped open. Did that mean Sadie was her companion now?

Before she could ask, Sadie spoke again. *We have to risk taking you into Dryton, but you are to keep your head down and talk to no one. All going well, we will be able to sneak through without anyone seeing us.*

'How big is the town? What if we can't find her?'

*The girl wore a green dress, meaning she is an Earth witch, and most likely a healer. I will be able to find her.* Sadie turned around and moved off.

Merry followed, finding the going much easier on more level ground, though she had to dodge around bushes and low obstacles the cat climbed over or under with ease. After an hour of walking, the valley narrowed and a worn path appeared in the trees. Merry was able to walk beside Sadie, and to ask a question that had been bugging her.

'Why does my grandmother have enemies?' What could she have done that would make people distrust or dislike any from her bloodline?

*She went against guild orders, refusing to allow them to control when and where she employed her magic. A warrant for her arrest was issued, and to avoid capture she fled to your world. She returned here years later, hoping the guild stranglehold on all witches and mages had eased, and that she could return with her son, only to find out they were even more in control. She was betrayed by another mage, and subsequently imprisoned by the guild. It took many years before she could free herself and return to your world.*

Sadie's mental voice was matter of fact, but it still gave Merry a chill. This explained why her grandmother had gone missing when Merry's father was a boy. So sad to think she had been prevented from returning. All their lives would have been very different if this guild had not interfered. Before she could ask more questions, about the guild and why they had imprisoned her grandmother, the path joined with a wide dirt road. On the other side of the road was a small town, though the buildings were nothing like what Merry was used to.

They were all relatively small, made of grey bricks, many of them with tiled roofs that peaked in a cone shape. They had small windows, and wooden doors with brass hinges. A cobbled road wound its way between the buildings, but Sadie veered to the left, towards the back of the nearest building.

*I will find you somewhere to wait out of sight, while I find the healer. The less you are seen, the better.*

Merry kept her head down, as she followed closely behind Sadie. There were people in the street to her left, the women wearing long dresses in drab colours, and the men in equally drab shirts and trousers. Their attire was all browns and greys, with some cream. Nothing like the emerald green dress of the woman Sadie had said was an Earth witch.

'You there, stop in the name of the Fairweather Guild.'

Merry hunched her shoulders and quickened her pace, hoping the booming voice was not directed at her.

'Stop.'

Despite her best efforts, Merry's feet stopped moving. She made to flee, but nothing happened. She could still move her upper body, but her legs and feet were frozen in place, as if some unseen force had clamped around them. Heart thudding in her chest, she looked for Sadie. The black cat was at the edge of the building, out of sight. The cat's eyes were wide, back arched.

In the periphery, Merry could see a young woman

with dark brown hair and a pronounced widow's peak storming towards her. The woman had one arm raised, hand clenched in a fist and pointed at Merry. Unlike the other townsfolk, she wore a fitted red robe, with silver and black braided trim around the cuffs and hem. Merry twisted her upper body to face her, not liking the avid way the woman stared at her. This woman's robe appeared to be made of a finer fabric than the clothes the other people in the street wore, and a silver sword pendant dangled from a thick chain hanging around her neck.

All the people in the vicinity had stopped whatever they'd been doing and now watched with matching looks of trepidation on their faces as the woman, who appeared to be a few years older than Merry, barrelled up to her.

A smug smile curved the woman's face. 'Meredith Meadows, did you really think this ridiculous costume and wearing a glamour to make you appear younger would stop me from recognising you? Enforcers are required to memorise the likeness of all guild traitors in their first year of training. I would never forget your face.'

Merry's eyes went wide. 'Ah, no, sorry, you've mistaken me for someone else.' She shook her head vehemently. 'I'm not who you think I am.'

The woman's brown eyes narrowed. 'I'm not stupid. Though you must be for coming back here. Whatever your reason, I can assure you, you will not escape a second time.'

Merry held up her hands, palms outward. 'Look, I get that you think you know who I am, but you really don't. I'm new here. I haven't betrayed anyone or escaped from anywhere.'

The woman leaned closer, stretching the hand that was not clenched into a fist towards Merry. 'Don't be-' her voice cut off when she touched Merry's face. A puzzled expression replaced the smugness of before as she snatched her hand back.

She tilted her head on the side as she unclenched her fist. 'You're not wearing a glamour. You really aren't Meredith. Who are you?'

Merry attempted a smile, relieved when she found she could now move her legs. 'I'm no one. Just passing through.' With that she ducked around the woman and headed for the corner of the building where she had last seen Sadie.

The black cat was waiting and quickly took off.

Merry raced after her, not looking back, scared she would find the woman chasing her. When Sadie finally stopped a couple of streets over, they were alone.

'Who was that?' Merry gasped out, struggling to catch her breath.

*I do not know her name, but her robe marks her as one of the guild's enforcers, and they are not fans of your grandmother.*

'Clearly.'

*Enforcers were responsible for guarding Meredith and others the guild considered as traitors. They would not have been pleased by her escape. For a young enforcer, to be the one to recapture Meredith would be a great boost to her reputation and standing.*

'Is she a witch or a mage?' Merry asked, remembering what Sadie had said earlier.

*Neither. Her ability, like all enforcers, is with the mental manipulation of physical objects. What is referred to in your world as telekinesis. When she reached for you and curled her hand into a fist, she was visualising an invisible band rendering you immobile, and her ability made that a reality. It is not magic such as what a witch or mage is capable of, but it makes enforcers like her perfect for subduing those who oppose the guild.*

'That explains why I couldn't move, then.' Merry shuddered, hoping she never had to come face to face with the nasty woman again. 'But why did she think I was my grandmother? I'm nineteen. My grandmother was in her sixties.'

*The use of magic can slow the ageing process. The stronger the magic, the less the body ages. Your grandmother was one of the most powerful mages of all time. If she had remained in Tirana, using her abilities, she would appear to be decades younger than she was. But magic is limited in your world. Certain areas are stronger than others or the portal we used would not exist. Her time there aged her considerably, but from the enforcer's words she believed you were using a glamour to make yourself appear younger. When she touched you, she would have realised her error. But now is not the time to discuss the limitations of glamour or the effects of magic on the lifespan of mages. I have tracked the healer. It is time to get the spell box back so we can get you out of here, before the enforcer realises you are your grandmother's descendant.*

The prompt was enough to silence Merry's remaining questions, and she quickly followed Sadie to a small building, one without a cone shaped roof. Above the doorway was a timber sign with a leaf carved into it. A bell tingled as Merry opened the door and entered. She shut the door as soon as Sadie was inside, and then looked around.

They were in a small shop filled with many different fragrances, all coming from tiny jars set on shelves along one wall. There was a small counter and behind that hung a green curtain.

The curtain pulled back and a young woman close to Merry's age stepped out with a welcoming smile. She wore an emerald green dress, and her thick black hair was tied back in a braid.

Merry hoped this was the woman they had seen with the chest.

The woman's smile dimmed as she looked at Merry, her brow creasing. 'May I help you?'

For a moment, Merry expected Sadie to speak, and then remembered the other woman wouldn't be able to hear her.

'I hope so. I lost a box, at the base of the hill,' she

waved a hand in the direction she thought the hill was, 'and I think you may have picked it up.'

The woman's eyebrows rose. 'That was your spell box? I wondered what it was doing there. Spell boxes are an expensive item to be abandoned like that.'

'Not abandoned. Lost,' said Merry, hoping the woman was not going to expect payment for the supposedly expensive box. She had no idea what they used for currency here in Tirana. 'I dropped it, and it rolled down the hill. I was on my way to pick it up, but you got there before me.'

The woman nodded and opened the curtain with one hand. 'I'll get it for you…' she moved into the room behind the curtain, her voice muffled as she said, 'though I am afraid the fall has broken the spell that was inside it.'

'Broken?' Merry looked to Sadie, who jumped up on the counter.

The woman returned with the spell box and set it on the counter, giving a slight nod to Sadie. 'Yes, but I am sure you will have no trouble fixing it.'

Merry gaped at her. Fix it? She wouldn't know the first thing about fixing a spell that had transported her to another world.

The woman's smile dropped. 'You must be able to fix it, if you are the mage who made the spell.' She placed a hand on the spell box, suspicion in her hazel eyes. 'You did make it, right?'

Merry's shoulder's slumped. 'My grandmother did. But she's dead, and I'm not a mage. I can't make spells.'

The woman looked from Merry to Sadie. 'But you have a familiar? This is your familiar, yes, not just a pet cat?'

*As if I would ever be a pet.* Sadie arched her back and swished her tail. *And I am a companion, not a familiar.*

Merry stifled a snort. 'Sadie prefers the term companion.'

The suspicion in the woman's eyes cleared a little. 'Oh, of course.' She dipped her head towards Sadie. 'My apologies.'

Sadie gave a regal nod, sitting on her haunches and wrapping her tail around her feet.

'Look,' said Merry, 'that is my grandmother's spell box. I just inherited it, but I am not a mage so I can't fix the spell. Would you be able to do it?'

A gasp of surprise came from the woman. 'Me? I'm only a witch, a healer at that,' she said, tapping a badge that was shaped like a leaf sewn on the left side of her bodice. 'And not a strong one or I'd be in mage training for the guild. A spell of this type is well beyond my abilities.'

Merry's stomach dropped. 'If you can't fix it, how am I supposed to get back to my world?'

The woman's eyes widened. 'Oh my, are you saying you're from the old world?'

Merry hesitated, not sure if she should divulge the truth. After a prompt from Sadie she gave a nod. 'Yes, but I came here by accident, and all I want to do is go home.'

The woman stared at Merry, one hand covering her mouth. Then she gave a shake. 'Well, to fix a spell of this complexity would require a mage from the guild. Hiring one of them would be extremely expensive though.'

A guild mage. Sadie had said the guild was her grandmother's enemy, and that enforcers like the one she had just met would arrest her if they knew she was of the same bloodline. It would be too dangerous to approach any other member of the guild, even if she had the money to pay.

'I can't afford to go to the guild. But there has to be someone else who could help me.'

The healer shook her head. 'I'm afraid not. Only a guild mage would have any hope of fixing or creating a spell to transport you back to your own world. Frankly, I'm not sure how many of them could create a spell this powerful. To part the veil between worlds, to allow safe passage, that is serious magic.'

Merry turned to look at Sadie, a sickening feeling growing in the pit of her stomach.

If what the healer said was true, they were going to be stuck in Tirana forever.

# CHAPTER 4

Merry slumped against the counter, blindly staring into the distance. How was she going to get home now?

Behind the counter, the healer cleared her throat. 'I'm sorry I can't help you.'

Tears pricked Merry's eyes, but she managed a small smile. 'Thanks.'

The healer held out her hand. 'I'm Ellen Hayland.'

Merry stifled a sigh and shook her hand. 'Merry,' she said. Then she looked away from the light of curiosity in Ellen's gaze.

'Are witches still hunted in your world? Is that why you're here?' Ellen asked, eyes gleaming. 'According to lore, our ancestors fled from there many generations ago to escape persecution. They created magical portals to allow them to travel to other worlds in search of safe haven.'

Merry shook her head. 'That was hundreds of years ago. People can be witches if they want.' She'd read about the witch hunts that had taken place in the middle ages and didn't blame Ellen's ancestors for fleeing, though none of the history books had mentioned anything about portals or real magic.

'That all took place in Europe though, not Australia where I come from, and you talk just like me,' said Merry. Ellen had a slight accent, but was speaking a more modern form of English than what Merry would have expected if she was descended from European witches.

*Portals exist all over your world, but those that led to Tirana from the old country were destroyed to prevent the witch hunters from following the refugees. Witches were able to travel back to your world via portals in other continents for many centuries, to places they would not be hunted, facilitating the sharing of knowledge and language, as well as to collect seeds and livestock for farming. Then, forty years ago, the guild decreed portal travel illegal and destroyed all the ones they could find, trapping many witches and mages on the other side. Your grandmother was fortunate they were not aware of the portal that led to Belwich as she used it twice to escape the guild. If she had not done so, you would never have been born.*

Sadie's swords explained why there was no language barrier, but from what she'd seen, life in Tirana was far different from what Merry was used to. The witches who fled here had clearly clung to their medieval way of life.

As if she was thinking along the same lines, Ellen asked, 'Is your world very different from Tirana?' She blushed as she waved a hand at Merry's clothes. 'It must be. No woman here would wear such revealing attire.'

Merry shrugged. 'This is normal, where I come from. Women can wear anything they want.' Well, in most countries anyway, and depending on the situation. She had felt underdressed while in the solicitor's office.

Ellen perked up. 'Anything? You are not required to wear clothes that display your magical ability?' This was asked with a wistful air.

'Huh?'

Ellen smiled. 'I must wear green to show an affinity with Earth magic. If I had the ability to shape wind, I would be required to wear white, for Air. Water is represented by wearing blue, orange for Fire, while those capable of wielding Spirit wear purple. There are witches and mages who have an affinity for more than one type of magic, though they mainly wear the colour that indicates where they are strongest. Mages, those who have completed their guild training and mastered their abilities, are required to wear robes that display the colour of their element, and to show that they are above us lowly witches. Then there are those who do not possess an elemental magic but are able to move objects with their minds. They must wear red robes.'

That explained the robe the enforcer was wearing.

Merry thought back to the other people she had seen when she had first entered Dryton. 'What does it mean if someone is wearing brown or grey?'

'That they have no magical ability and are lower class. The nobility can wear either black with silver or cream and gold,' said Ellen, as she pointed at Merry's hair. 'To wear a colour and to not have an affinity for that kind of magic could see you arrested by the guild enforcers. If you do not wish to attract their attention, you would be wise to colour your hair.'

Merry tucked the wayward purple strands that had come out of her bun back beneath the makeshift head wrap. 'I've already had one run in with an enforcer. I do not want to have another.' But she didn't plan on staying in Tirana long enough to warrant dyeing her hair, though it was ironic it would cause her as much trouble here as it did back home, at least according to her parents.

Ellen's eyes widened. 'What happened?'

'She mistook me for someone else,' said Merry. Remembering Sadie's warning to keep a low profile, she figured it would be best not to mention her grandmother's name. Ellen was being friendly now, but what would she do if she realised Merry was the granddaughter of a guild traitor?

Ellen was peering intently at her. Then she clapped a hand over her mouth. 'Oh my living stars, you're Meredith Meadows. I can't believe I didn't recognise you, even with purple hair. My mentor has a picture of you from when you were in guild training together. You look exactly like you did then.' She tilted her head to one side, a puzzled expression creasing her face. 'Though I can't detect the glamour you are using to appear younger, and why would you need someone else to fix a broken spell?'

Merry shook her head. 'There's no glamour, and I'm not who you think I am.'

Ellen snorted. 'Of course it's you. I'm surprised the enforcer let you go. They have orders to arrest you on sight.'

So much for hiding who she was related to. 'You don't understand, the Meredith Meadows they are looking for is not me. It's my grandmother.'

'Your grandmother?' Ellen frowned.

'Yes. I never met her, but I gather I look just like her. She's dead now, and I accidentally triggered her spell, the one that brought me here, and now I need to find a way home before the guild try to arrest me again.'

Ellen's eyes widened. 'Oh dear.'

'I'm not a mage, and when the enforcer touched me, she realised I wasn't my grandmother. But Sadie tells me I'll be in big trouble when they figure out that we are related, and I need to get home before that happens.' Home, so she could sell the bookshop and forget it contained a portal that led to another world. She'd go straight to the solicitor's office, sign the contract and let *Huntington Inc.* deal with it all. Though, if they needed the spell box to use the portal then they need never know it existed. Merry planned to bury it in the deepest hole she could find.

'Yes,' said Ellen, a thoughtful expression on her face. 'The guild will be very interested in you, seeing as you are a Meadows mage.'

'I told you, I'm not a mage.'

Ellen gave her a wry grin. 'If you weren't a mage, or had no potential to become one, the spell wouldn't have brought you here, and you wouldn't be able to hear your familiar's mental voice.'

*I am a companion, not a familiar.*

Merry grimaced at Ellen's words, ignoring Sadie's grumbled complaint. That was two people who had told her the same thing, but she wasn't a mage. She couldn't do magic or cast spells. There had to be another explanation. Not that it mattered. All she wanted was to go home.

She turned to Ellen. 'Please, you must know of someone who can fix the spell, someone who isn't connected to the guild. I can't stay here. I have to get home. My parents will be looking for me.' Her dad's life had been thrown into chaos when his mother had disappeared. What would he do when he realised Merry had vanished as well?

Ellen bit at her bottom lip, her gaze flicking from Merry to Sadie and back again. After a long moment she gave a sigh. 'There is someone who may be able to help you, but I need you to promise me that you will tell no one who she is or where she's hiding. If the guild finds her, they will force her to join them, as they would do with you.'

Merry nodded. 'Of course. I'll do anything.'

'Very well. I often have to leave to perform healing, so no one will think it amiss if I close the shop early today. First though, I will gather some supplies for our journey.' She scanned Merry. 'I will also find you something else to wear. You are going to attract far too much attention dressed like that.'

Ellen scooped up the spell box and headed back through the curtain, beckoning for Merry to follow her. She stepped into a large space that had to be where Ellen lived as well as worked. A small timber bed was shoved against one wall, while the other was filled with benches and shelving, presumably where Ellen made the items she sold in her shop. A small table with two chairs occupied the middle of the room.

In a whirl of activity, Ellen stuffed a number of items from the shelves into a pack, including the spell box, and then she rummaged in a wooden chest at the foot of the bed, pulling out items of clothing.

Minutes later Merry wore a dress in the same shade of green as the one Ellen wore, though in a slightly different style. The one Ellen had on was more fitted in the bodice and then tapered out into a full skirt, and had long, narrow sleeves, while Merry's sleeves were flowing, but the dress was more fitted. Her old clothes were stuffed into her bag, though she still wore the wrap to hide her hair. Ellen secured a leather pouch around her waist and then led the way to the front of the store. Merry slung her bag over her shoulder and then touched the badge on the front of the dress, a gold leaf the same as the one carved into the sign.

'What does this mean?' Merry asked as she stepped outside and Ellen locked the door behind her.

'It is the sign for a healer,' said Ellen as she scanned the street. She held up a hand for silence, then directed Merry to follow her as she stepped off the sidewalk and onto the cobbled roadway.

Sadie slipped along in the shadows of the buildings as Ellen led them to the edge of Dryton, in the opposite direction to the one Merry had entered by. There were a few people about, some of them greeting Ellen. The young witch did not stop, and Merry kept her head down, hoping no one would take too close a look and mistake her for her grandmother. If Ellen knew what she looked like, other townsfolk might as well, and that enforcer could still be lurking around. Shoulders hunched, expecting to be outed at any moment, Merry did not speak until they had left Dryton behind them.

They had left the cobbled road and now trod a dirt path as Merry raised her head, scanning the trees to either side to make sure no one was lurking nearby, before asking, 'The person you are taking me to see, why does the guild want her?'

Ellen heaved a sigh, gesturing for Merry to leave the path and follow her into the trees on the left before answering. 'She is a powerful Spirit mage, and by law she must be a member of the guild, sworn to uphold their rules. But she believes no one person should control what a mage, or witch, does with their magic, and she refused. She has been hunted by the guild ever since, just as they will hunt for you once they find out who you are.'

A chill swept over Merry at Ellen's words and she went silent as they wound their way through a large wood. There was no set path here, and their pace slowed. Sadie bounded in from the left, stalking a butterfly, making Merry smile, but it soon dimmed as more questions crowded her head.

'Why does the guild insist people have to join them?'

'It goes back to the war, I think. It was before my time, when mages like my mentor and your grandmother were our age. Back then Tirana was ruled by a king, Reagan of Lakehold, who used mages to keep his subjects in line. A powerful mage, Ophelia Fairweather, started the guild to safeguard the rights of mages, giving them an alternative from becoming enslaved by the king. From what I've been told, she gathered up as many of the more powerful mages as she could and then demanded King Reagan release the ones he had in servitude. He refused and declared war on the guild. But the guild won, and the tower was built over the ruins of King Reagan's castle.'

Ellen lifted the hem of her dress and stepped over a fallen tree trunk before continuing her explanation. 'Debra, my mentor and the one I'm taking you to see, said that after the war Ophelia became obsessed with making sure no mage was ever forced to work for the king or any of the other nobles that came to power after he was defeated. She determined the best way to protect them all was by making them members of the guild. But somewhere along the way she became almost as bad as King Reagan. When people like Debra and your grandmother questioned the direction the guild was taking, she refused to listen, demanding their obedience. They fled the guild, along with many others, and she has her enforcers hunting them down.'

'If this Ophelia is so concerned about protecting all magic users why aren't you, and the rest of the witches, part of the guild?'

'I'm not powerful enough. She is only interested in magic users like your grandmother, who have mastery of one or more elements, or those born with enforcer magic. Potential mages like you, who have a familiar, sorry, companion,' she ducked her head towards Sadie, 'can do stronger spells than me. I'm able to heal minor injuries, like bruises or sprains, but anything else requires a mage. And anyone seeking the services of a guild mage has to pay for the privilege, so ordinary people have little chance of doing so. Only the wealthy can afford the payment. All towns under guild protection must pay a tithe to the guild, and witches like me have to give a share of any money we receive from using our abilities. If not, we would be arrested, our possessions stripped from us, and be banned from ever practising magic again.'

Ellen shook her head. 'Debra said the birth rate among witches as well as mages has been declining, with the strength of the inherited magic less in each successive generation. She said that if the guild stranglehold on our magic is not lifted soon, a day may come when no babies will be born with magic. Even with the slowed rate of ageing for those strong enough to be guild mages, their bloodlines will eventually die out and then magic will be lost to Tirana.'

'That's horrible. Doesn't Ophelia Fairweather care that her guild will be responsible for a world without magic?'

'She didn't believe Debra or your grandmother, or any of the others who have tried to warn her. She is convinced what she is doing is right, but she's wrong, even if it doesn't lead to the end of magic.' Ellen shook her head, distress thickening her voice. 'Hundreds of people have died, crops failed, their livelihoods destroyed, all because they couldn't afford to pay for a powerful Earth mage to help them. Life under King Reagan may have been hard, but at least then more people had the chance of hiring a mage when they needed to. Ophelia and the guild need to be stopped but she is too strong. The oaths she has used to bind the mages to the guild makes it impossible for them to go against her, and ones like Debra are too few to make a difference.'

Ellen sighed. 'I had hoped that one day your grandmother would rally those that are still in hiding and that they would wrest control of the guild from Ophelia, but with her dead then there is no one left that is strong enough to even think about fighting back. Unless...' She glanced over at Merry.

'Don't look at me,' she said, shaking her head and holding her hands up in front of her. 'I don't know the first thing about magic. I may be able to hear Sadie, but that's it. I just want to go home, not take on an entire guild.' One run in with an enforcer was more than enough.

Ellen gave a sad nod, and for a long time neither of them spoke. An hour later the young witch called a halt beside a slow-moving creek, scanning the bushes that surrounded the small clearing they were in.

The clearing was hemmed in by trees, one of them toppled sideways, roots exposed and the topmost branches almost reaching to the creek. Sunlight filtered through the standing trees, creating a dappled pattern on thick grass. It was quiet, peaceful and serene, and Merry breathed in a lungful of the fresh air. Then she stretched out the kinks in her leg muscles, not used to walking for such a long period of time, or in this kind of terrain, though she was pleased she'd chosen to wear her ankle boots instead of sandals that morning.

Sadie, showing no signs of wear from the walk, slipped between Ellen and Merry and headed to the creek edge, leaning forward to delicately lap at the water. The water looked clear and inviting, and Merry was contemplating joining the cat when Ellen spoke.

'We can rest here for a while,' she said, as she pulled out a package from her pack and opened it up. Inside were two thick slabs of homemade bread, slathered with butter. She handed one to Merry.

Not realising until then how hungry she was, her appetite having vanished during the portal trip from Belwich to Tirana, Merry sat with her back against the fallen tree and quickly polished off the bread. It was delicious, though plain. Ellen sat beside her and ate her own bread and then she retrieved two timber mugs from her bag. She headed to the creek and knelt to scoop water into both mugs and then returned to where Merry was sitting.

Ellen placed the mugs on the grass between them and then reached into the pouch tied around her waist, this time pulling out a small leather satchel and unwrapping it. As she spread the satchel on the grass the scent of dried herbs tickled Merry's nose. The inside of the satchel was lined with pockets, and as she watched, Ellen opened one and the herb scent grew stronger. Ellen reached inside the pocket and pulled out a pinch of herbs, which she sprinkled in both of the mugs. Then she placed one hand on her chest and the other in the air over the mugs, eyes closed for a moment, as she murmured something beneath her breath.

Goose bumps spread over Merry's arms.

The sensation faded as Ellen opened her eyes and

handed Merry one of the cups. 'It will be fine to drink now.'

Merry peered into her mug. There was no sign of the herbs Ellen had added to the creek water. She lifted the mug and took a sip, eyes widening at the refreshing taste of the water. She quickly emptied the mug, her taste-buds tingling and a rush of energy surging through her body.

'What was that?' Merry placed the mug back on the grass, watching on as Ellen took out a water skin and went to fill it from the creek before then stowing it in her pack. When the healer returned to sit beside her, Merry could still feel the tingle on the tip of her tongue, even as the aches in her legs seemed to recede.

Ellen gave a shrug. 'It's a simple spell, one designed to purify the water and give us some energy. We still have a fair way to travel before we reach Debra's cottage. It will be dark before we get there if we go any slower than we have been.'

Merry was impressed. From the way she now felt, she'd be able to run all night if she had to. And Ellen had said she wasn't a very powerful witch. 'That's a handy spell.'

'It can be, but it's not something we can take often. I want us to get as far away from Dryton as possible, in case that enforcer you met decides to follow us,' said Ellen as she packed the satchel of herbs back into her pouch and put the mugs away in her pack.

Merry grimaced. 'I hope not.' She never wanted to

see that woman again, or any other enforcer. The sooner they got to Ellen's mentor and she could find a way home the better. With Ellen's magic water washing away her tiredness, it was time to get moving.

She looked around the small clearing for Sadie. The black cat was sitting in the shade of a tree on the other side of the clearing, delicately grooming herself. As Merry watched, the cat stiffened, head swinging around.

*Run!*

At Sadie's mental shout, Merry scrambled to her feet.

'What is it?' Ellen asked, slinging her pack over her shoulder as she jumped up. 'What's wrong?'

Before Merry had a chance to answer, she caught a glimpse of red through the trees.

The enforcer. It had to be.

Another flash of red came from the left and Merry spun to see a man dressed in an enforcer robe running towards her. At his side was a young man who wore black trousers under a robe that had panels of blue and white. A gasp came from beside her and she turned to see Ellen staring at yet another man in an enforcer robe on their right, even as the woman who had accosted Merry in Dryton stepped into the clearing.

Three enforcers, and what had to be a mage with mastery of both Air and Water magic seeing as he was dressed in a robe of blue and white.

Merry tried to flee, but before she had taken a step something clamped around her entire body, and she was wrenched to a standstill.

Beside her, Ellen was also struggling to move.

Frozen in place, Merry could do nothing as they were surrounded.

The female enforcer stepped forward, fist raised, a smug expression on her face as she surveyed Merry and Ellen. 'Now, where were you two off to, I wonder.'

Merry said nothing, conscious of another enforcer stepping to the side of Ellen, his clenched fist also raised. He had to be using his ability to hold her in place, as the woman was doing to her.

Beside her, she heard Ellen take a deep breath. 'We were out gathering herbs, mistress, for our remedies.'

The female enforcer looked over at Merry, gaze dropping to her borrowed green dress. 'So, you're supposed to be a healer?'

Merry lifted her chin and fought to keep her expression blank as she said, 'Yes.'

'Well then, in that case you should have no trouble seeing to this.' She pulled back the sleeve of her right arm and displayed a scratch on her wrist.

Merry stared at it, unblinking, not knowing what to do.

'My apprentice is still learning to master her abilities, mistress. Allow me to assist you,' said Ellen.

The woman didn't respond to the offer, never taking her eyes off Merry. 'Even a healer with barely a spark of magic, or training, would be able to heal this paltry scratch. So, heal me.'

'Kassandra, that is enough.'

Merry couldn't move her head to see who spoke, but the young man in the blue and white robe stepped into her line of sight. He was tall, handsome, with light grey eyes and wavy brown hair that curled around his ears. While the enforcers all wore sword pendants, he had a round medallion that shimmered in the light, with a pattern that seemed to move of its own accord. It reminded Merry of clouds moving across the sky and her fingers itched to reach out and trace the pattern, to learn its shape.

She tore her eyes away from it and focused on his face instead. Unlike Kassandra and the male enforcers, he bore a friendly expression. Merry shifted under his gaze but forced herself to maintain eye contact. If she acted like someone with nothing to hide, maybe he would start to believe it. From what she had observed so far, he was the one in charge.

'Release them,' he said, a note of command in his voice.

'Master Fairweather, they may try to escape,' Kassandra said, a cruel light in her eyes suggesting she wished they would try.

'Are you saying you and your brethren would be unable to stop them if they were to attempt an escape?' The young man's lips curved in a slight smile.

Kassandra flushed, and shot a dirty glance at Merry, but the enforcer released her clenched fist and the pressure holding her immobile vanished.

Merry stumbled, and the young man reached out to

steady her, his hand firm on her arm as his smile widened.

'I apologise if we startled you and your friend, but it appears you have sparked the interest of Miss Piermont here. Tell me, what is your name?'

'Ahhh...' Merry shot a glance at Ellen. Her grandmother was known as Meredith. Would they recognise Merry as being a derivative of that?

To be on the safe side, she gave her middle name and added on her mother's maiden name. 'My name is Lee Harrison. And you are?'

'Gabriel Fairweather, and I am pleased to meet you… Lee Harrison.' The way he said the name made her think he knew it was a lie. Well, sort of a lie.

To cover any sign of guilt, she waved a hand at Ellen and introduced her. But like Kassandra, Gabriel apparently had no interest in her new friend. His eyes remained on Merry, a considering look in his light grey gaze. Given how good looking he was, and the nice way he filled out his robe, Merry wouldn't have minded having the attention of someone like him under normal circumstances. But with the last name of Fairweather and three enforcers at his back, she didn't think he was here to flirt with her.

A quick glance around the clearing showed no sign of Sadie, and the cat's mental voice was silent. With luck, she was well hidden. Merry and Ellen had to get away from this lot so they could find the cat and get out of there. The buzz from the magic water thrummed inside her body still, assuring her she had the energy needed to sprint away when the opportunity presented itself. But, when she looked over at Kassandra, the cruel set to her features made Merry's heart race. It wouldn't be so easy to get away from the enforcer a second time.

She looked back to Gabriel, hoping against hope that she was wrong. 'It is nice to meet you, but Ellen and I need to go. We have herbs to collect, remedies to make, so if you will excuse us.'

She made to walk around him, but Kassandra stepped into her path, stopping her from leaving the clearing, a threat evident in the clenching of her fists and narrowed eyes. The other enforcers had stepped closer as well, hemming Merry and Ellen in.

'You bear a striking resemblance to a witch by the name of Meredith Meadows. By chance, do you know her?' Gabriel's tone was even, but still, there was something in it, a hint of concern.

Merry met his gaze, glad she could truthfully say, 'No, I have never met her.'

'She's lying,' said Kassandra, chin jutting forward.

Gabriel shook his head. 'No, I don't believe she is.' He fixed his gaze on Merry as he leaned in closer and placed a hand on her arm again. 'But I do believe you know of her.'

Warmth spread through Merry at his closeness, all too aware of his intent gaze. She struggled to keep her expression blank and her voice even as she said, 'I'd never heard of her before today.' That statement was also true.

Kassandra sucked in a breath. 'That is not possible. No one in Tirana could make that claim.'

'And yet, once again, I believe... Miss Harrison is telling the truth.'

Merry stifled a grimace at the way Gabriel stressed the name again. She was in so much trouble. She clutched her shoulder bag close to her body, gritting her teeth, sure she was about to be arrested.

The thought had barely formed before Gabriel stepped back and waved towards Ellen. 'You may go, Miss Hayland. The guild has no interest in witches. But you,' he said as he turned back to Merry, 'are of great interest to the guild. You will need to come with us. My aunt will be very interested to meet someone who says she has no knowledge of Meredith Meadows, while being almost identical to a younger version of Tirana's most infamous mage.'

Before Merry could say anything, he waved a hand and her legs were once more clamped down by an invisible force. She could do nothing as Kassandra moved in, wrenched her hands behind her back and used a thin cord to bind her wrists together. The force holding her still vanished, but Kassandra kept a firm hold on the other end of the rope, looping it around her wrist, making sure Merry was not going anywhere without her.

Ellen, with a terrified glance towards Merry, fled the

clearing. Merry didn't blame her for getting out of there, not after what she'd said about the guild. But it still stung to know how quickly she had abandoned her.

A streak of black shot through the trees behind Ellen, and the sting intensified when she realised Sadie had deserted her as well. Now what was she was going to do? She'd lost her only allies and was going to be taken to the very place Sadie had said she had to avoid at all cost.

'There's no point heading back to town now. We'll stop here for the night and meet up with the others in the morning,' said Gabriel, scanning the clearing.

As the other two enforces began setting up camp, Merry's spirits sank even further.

How was she going to get out of this mess?

With her hands tied behind her, affecting her balance, Merry stumbled over to the fallen tree and sat on it with her back to the others. The rope went tight, making her wince, and she looked back to see Kassandra tugging on the end wrapped around her own wrist and with a sour look on her face. Merry glared at her and then turned away, gazing into the trees, hoping she would see something that would help her escape.

A flash of movement low to the ground had her spirits rising, and she smiled as a cat sidled through the shadows on the other side of a nearby clump of bushes. Sadie had come back.

But when the cat came up around the bush, she realised it wasn't her grandmother's companion. This cat had sleek dark grey fur, with white on the tips of its paws and under the chin, and light green eyes. It came close and sniffed at her foot before bounding over the fallen tree. Merry turned to watch as it stalked over to where Gabriel was helping one of the male enforcers pitch a red canvas tent.

Gabriel had taken off his robe, the sleeveless white undershirt and form-hugging black trousers high-lighting a fit body. His arms were tanned, very nicely shaped, the muscles flexing with each movement. All the enforcers still wore their red robes, sweat coating the face of the one unrolling a roll of red canvas on the ground on the other side of the tent Gabriel was working on. Kassandra had not moved and still had her gaze fixed on Merry.

Merry ignored the dark stare the enforcer was shooting her way as she watched the cat reach Gabriel and rub against his leg. He bent down and said some-thing to the cat. She couldn't hear what he said, but she had no trouble hearing the cat's response.

*They are camped at the northern edge of the forest, their mission as successful as yours, and will remain there until you join them.* The cat twisted its head and stared unblink-ingly at Merry. *Your aunt will be pleased.*

Gabriel's aunt might be pleased, but Merry wasn't. She had to get out of there, and if no one else was around to help her, she had to figure out how to escape on her own.

Soon both tents were up, and Merry's hands were untied so she could have something to eat. She wasn't hungry, thanks to the food Ellen had given her earlier, but made a show of eating slowly to stave off the moment when she would be bound again. It was a good thing she had no appetite. The hard biscuits and canteen of water weren't all that appetising. The water Ellen had magicked had tasted way better, and so had the bread. But she murmured a thank you when Gabriel gave it to her and nibbled on the hard biscuit as she scanned the others. Kassandra was still standing beside Merry, waiting to bind her wrists once she had eaten.

Merry's wrists stung from the short amount of time she had already been tied up, and she had no intention of allowing it to happen a second time. She cast Kassandra what she hoped was a pleasant smile.

'I need to go to the bathroom,' she said in a quiet voice, not wanting to announce it to the men.

Kassandra's eyes narrowed. 'I don't believe you.'

Merry worked to maintain her smile as she pointed to the canteen at her feet. 'Doesn't matter if you believe me or not. I need to go. Water has that effect on me.'

Kassandra heaved a sigh and then, never taking her eyes off Merry, called out in a loud voice, 'The girl said she needs to empty her bladder.' Then she indicated for Merry to follow her as she strode towards a stand of trees a short distance from the clearing.

Merry, face flushing, avoided looking at Gabriel or the others as she picked up the hem of her long dress and followed Kassandra. She had no real plan, hoping that something would occur to her as she went. They were only a short distance from the camp, behind a second stand of trees, when Kassandra came to a halt and turned to Merry.

'Go there. Don't try anything. I'll be watching.' She pointed at a nearby bush, and then folded her arms over her chest and glared at Merry.

Merry glared right back at her. 'You could at least turn around.'

Kassandra stiffened. 'No.'

With another glare, Merry scanned the bush the enforcer had pointed at. She moved around it and found a small space that she could bend down in. She hadn't been lying when she'd said she needed to use the bathroom. It was awkward, with the dress bunched around her waist, and her bag still slung across her body, but she managed as best she could. Never a fan of camping at the best of times, having to relieve herself in the middle of nowhere, with no toilet paper and no way to wash her hands, and an antagonistic stranger watching on, would make anyone's bladder shy. Goose bumps rippled across her skin as she contemplated having to do this on a regular basis.

She avoided looking in the enforcer's direction when she finished and straightened up. She stepped around the bush, and gasped to find Kassandra slumped against a tree, eyes closed.

'Hurry up, she won't remain asleep for long.'

Merry twisted to see Ellen waving to her from behind the tree against which the enforcer was propped. Relief thrummed through her as she made her way around the tree and found Sadie waiting there as well. They hadn't abandoned her after all. With a motion to be quiet, Ellen set off in a direction that took them away from the clearing. Merry hurried after her, expecting to hear an outcry as Gabriel and the other enforcers discovered she'd escaped.

For a long moment, nothing happened and then shouts rose behind them. Merry increased her pace, almost running into Ellen's back. Soon the shouts grew fainter. Still, Merry did not allow herself to relax until they were well away from the clearing and had been unable to hear her former captors for some time.

'We can slow down now,' said Ellen.

Merry's muscles were thankful for the decrease in speed, as were her lungs. She'd never had so much physical activity in years, not since being forced to join in with school sports. The buzz from Ellen's magic water had long since worn off and her breath came in short gasps as her lungs worked overtime.

When she had enough breath to speak, she said, 'Thank you, both of you.' She looked down to where Sadie easily kept pace with them, the little cat giving no sign the run had winded her.

*You didn't truly believe we would abandon you, did you?*

With an inward wince for having had thoughts of abandonment, Merry said, 'I was worried something had happened to you both.'

'Sadie kept watch on the camp, waiting for the right time to stage a rescue, but we would never have managed it if you hadn't drawn the female enforcer away from the others,' said Ellen. 'There was no way I would have been able to put four people to sleep. It was hard enough to do one, with her being so alert.'

'I thought you couldn't hear Sadie?'

Ellen gave a wry laugh as she rubbed her left wrist. 'She got her point across, without words.'

Merry looked at the cat. 'You bit Ellen?'

*How else was I to make her understand that I needed her to stay put while I scouted the area?*

Merry shook her head at the lack of remorse in Sadie's mental voice, and then turned to Ellen. 'That is so cool, that you could put Kassandra to sleep. I had no idea how I was going to escape otherwise.'

Ellen shot her a small smile. 'You could probably learn it too. Mages who are able to communicate with a familiar are often able to master more than one discipline.'

Merry frowned. Gabriel had a familiar, and his robe suggested he had both Wind and Air magic. What else would he be capable of? A flush swept over her when the thought prompted a memory of his tanned arms, muscles on display as he helped to set up the tent. She tripped over a tree root and righted herself. The shadows were deepening around them, making it harder to spot potential obstacles. Not that it had been the shadows that had distracted her just then.

She cleared her throat and banished the image of Gabriel from her mind before asking, 'Is it much further? We won't be able to see where we're going, soon. Unless you can conjure up a light, as well as turn water into an energy drink and make people go to sleep.' She could do with more of Ellen's energy water right now, a yawn creeping up on her.

'I'm afraid light spells are out of my depth. My skills are with strengthening the effects of herbs and in curing minor ailments. That was how I put Kassandra to sleep, by using a spell to ease pain. But don't worry, we are almost there.'

Their pace had slowed as darkness fell, but soon a light appeared through gaps in the trees ahead of them. Ellen increased her speed and Merry followed along, eager to get out of the dark and find a way back to her own world. She just hoped Ellen's mentor would be able to fix the spell box so she could go home.

Ahead of her, Ellen gave a low cry as she edged past the final stand of trees and started to run. Merry stumbled over tree roots, grass tangling around her legs as she raced after her. Soon she burst out of the trees and into a clearing only slightly larger than the one they had stopped in earlier. A tiny cottage with stone walls and a sloping tiled roof was on the other side, a flickering light apparent through the splinters that were all that remained of the the front door. Ellen burst inside and gave another cry, and Merry ran the short distance to the door.

The flickering light came from dying embers in a fireplace, but that wasn't what caught Merry's attention.

The cottage consisted of one room, with the interior a jumble of broken furniture.

'What happened here?' Merry stepped around the remains of a small timber table and joined Ellen as she peered behind a curtain that was half pulled over one wall. A neatly made bed was set up in a small nook behind the curtain, the only item of furniture in the tiny cottage that wasn't broken or scattered on the stone floor. Colourful pillows and blankets were on the bed, and a pottery vase containing bright yellow flowers rested on a windowsill above the bedhead.

Ellen returned to the centre of the room and spun in a slow circle. Then she froze, peering down at something on the floor in front of the fireplace. She reached down and scooped it up, her face pale as she turned to Merry and held out a broken chain with a silver sword pendant dangling from it.

'The guild has her,' said Ellen, crumpling to the floor, sobs racking her slim frame.

Sadie wound through Merry's legs and surveyed the shambles the enforcers had left. *If the guild has already been here, it will be safe for the moment, but I would not recommend we linger longer than necessary.*

Merry gave a nod before kneeling down and wrapping her arms around her new friend, while Sadie poked her nose into the corners of the room. She thought back to when she had been captured, and what the grey and white cat that had sidled up to Gabriel had said.

'There are more guild people camped at the northern

edge of the forest,' she said. 'They're waiting there for Gabriel and the others to join them tomorrow morning. Maybe they're the ones who took her.'

Ellen scrambled free of Merry's arms, wiping the tears from her face with the back of her sleeve. 'We have to rescue her. If they take her back to the guild tower, she'll never be free.'

Sadie's body twitched. *We have no idea how many enforcers we would face. It would be madness to attempt a rescue.*

Merry didn't like the idea of going up against a second group of enforcers either, but if Ellen was right in thinking her mentor would know of a way to fix the spell box, it was a risk she had to take. 'We'll help you,' she said. *We have no choice.*

She wasn't sure if Sadie heard the mental comment at first, as the black cat gave a shake and then stalked towards the doorway of the cottage with her tail swishing from side to side. Then she stopped on the threshold and looked back at Merry, eyes glowing in the dying light from the fire.

*Indeed.*

Expression firming with determination, Ellen strode around the cottage, slinging off her pack and stuffing various items into it. Some of it was food, but others looked to be jars similar to what she'd had in the shelves in her shop. Last of all, she snatched a lantern off the wall and lit it with a twig she placed in the embers of the fire.

Then she turned to Merry. 'If we hurry, we can get to the edge of the forest before midnight.'

Merry gave one last look at the bed before following Ellen out of the cottage. She was exhausted and wanted nothing more than to curl up and sleep for a week, but finding Ellen's mentor and getting her to fix the broken spell had to come first.

They set off, the lantern providing just enough light to illuminate three paces ahead of them through the trees. Neither of them spoke as they walked, and Sadie was also silent, for which Merry was grateful. So much had happened since the moment she'd found out about her grandmother that she'd had little time to process it all. The questions were piling up in her head, but she wasn't sure if she would like any answers she received so she remained silent.

Besides, for all she knew Gabriel and the others were still out there searching for her. It was better to be quiet. Probably better to not have a lantern to signal to anyone nearby that people were about, but without it they would be completely in the dark.

Owls hooted high up in the trees, and a chill wind blew through the branches, making Merry glad Ellen had loaned her the dress. It was much warmer than her shorts and t-shirt would have been, while her socks and boots kept her feet warm.

The wind pushed and pulled at Merry, whipping strands of her hair free from the bun she had secured it in, and despite the warmth of her borrowed clothes she shivered. Moments later a wet drop landed on the tip of her nose. It was quickly followed by another, and then dozens more.

From one second to the next, a downpour appeared, soaking her through almost instantly.

'We're going to have to find shelter,' Ellen said as she turned around, the light of the lantern allowing Merry to see the frustration in her expression.

Ellen handed Merry the lantern and then placed a hand on a nearby tree. She put her other hand on her chest and closed her eyes, once again murmuring under her breath.

Goose bumps swept over Merry, while rain slipped down the neckline of her dress, adding to her discomfort as she shielded the lantern as best she could.

Ellen opened her eyes. 'There is a large tree we can shelter under that way,' she said as she pointed to the right of them. Keeping one hand on her chest and brushing her hand against the trees trunks they passed, Ellen led them to a huge tree that had a deep hollow in the ground between its roots. Ellen ushered Merry and Sadie into the hollow and then followed them in.

It was cramped, damp and cold, but better than being out in the storm. The wind was picking up, roaring through the trees and shaking the branches, even as the rain got heavier, creating a cacophony of noise that made it almost impossible to think, let alone to hear someone approaching. As the lantern sputtered and died, Merry could only hope the enforcers were also forced to seek shelter and wouldn't be out looking for them in this weather.

Huddled together with Ellen, some warmth returned to Merry's body, especially when Sadie curled up on her lap. Of them all, the cat seemed to be the most comfortable. Eyes closing, Merry drifted off to the sound of the wind and rain, her shivers slowly subsiding.

It seemed she had only just closed her eyes when she was jostled awake and opened her eyes to see Ellen slipping out of the hollow. Sadie was no longer on her lap, the rain had finally stopped, and a dim light shone through gaps in the trees around them.

'It will be dawn soon. We need to get moving. We need to find Debra and rescue her before Gabriel Fairweather and his enforcers arrive to bolster their numbers,' said Ellen, urgency throbbing in her voice.

Merry pushed the last vestiges of sleep from her brain and clambered out of the hollow, grimacing at the dampness that remained in the dress clinging to her skin. Her boots had kept her feet relatively dry, but she was sure they would be wrinkled like prunes if she were to remove her socks.

After taking care of a full bladder, she returned to Ellen's side and they set off through the trees, boots catching in the sodden earth. Her stomach grumbled, but the determination in Ellen's steps kept Merry from asking her if there was time to eat any of the food she had taken from the cottage. After they had rescued Debra, if they rescued her, she could see if there was a better time for them to eat something. A cup of water would be good too, to wash away the dryness in her mouth. She would also love a steaming hot cup of coffee, as well as a tube of toothpaste, a real toilet, and clean and dry clothes. Merry sighed as she thought of all the things she had taken for granted before this trip to another world.

As they walked, the trees around them thinned, as did the underbrush, and Ellen held up a finger to her lip. Not that they had been talking. Merry was still too tired to even think about carrying on a conversation and her muscles were aching, while Ellen had to be worried about her mentor. Sadie could talk to Merry any time she wanted, as no one else would be able to hear her, but it seemed the cat also chose silence.

Up ahead, Ellen stopped, tension in her frame, and Merry stepped lightly until she joined her and looked to see what had gained her attention.

Through a gap in the trees she caught two flashes of red. These proved to be tents like the ones Gabriel and his enforcers had been setting up before she'd escaped. There was no sign of people, friendly or otherwise, as Ellen and Merry crept closer. With two tents to choose from, how were they to know which one held Ellen's mentor?

*Wait here.* Sadie slunk in front of Merry.

Merry reached out, tapped Ellen on the arm and pointed to the cat.

Ellen gave a nod, crouching down as she watched the

black cat stealthily wind her way towards the tents. Soon she disappeared from sight.

Minutes later, Sadie returned. She was not alone.

Scampering along behind her was a brown and white rat. It ran up to Ellen and clambered onto her shoulder, nuzzling her cheek.

*Debra is in the second tent. There are two female enforcers in there with her, one of which is awake and on guard duty, while a male is sleeping in the other tent.*

Merry quietly relayed Sadie's words to Ellen.

Ellen's face, that had brightened at the arrival of the rat, fell. 'How are we going to get her out?'

*I've chewed through the rope binding Debra's wrists and let her know you are here. I need you to create a diversion so she can slip away in the confusion.*

It took Merry a moment to realise the squeaky new voice came from the rat. Its nose twitched as it stared at her.

'What kind of diversion?' Merry asked.

Ellen gasped, looking from Merry to the rat and then back again. 'You can hear Benny?'

'Yes. He said he's chewed through Debra's ropes, but needs a diversion before she can escape. But maybe you can make the enforcer who is awake go to sleep, the way you did with Kassandra.'

Ellen's eyes were wide, but she gave a nod. 'I'll need to get closer, and Benny will have to go back to tell Debra what we are planning.'

The rat jumped down from Ellen's shoulder and

scurried back to the guild camp, Sadie close on his heels. Merry followed Ellen around the perimeter of the camp, getting as close to the tent containing Debra as possible. When they were in position, Ellen placed a hand on her chest and closed her eyes, lips moving though Merry could not hear what she was saying.

Merry rubbed at the goose bumps that appeared on her arms as she peered at the tent, waiting to see if their plan was working. A soft rustle came from the back of the tent and it lifted up just enough to allow the rat to scamper out. He was immediately followed by Sadie, and then the head of a woman with grey tinged blonde hair emerged. She shimmied under the edge of the tent, moving just as quietly as the rat and cat had. When she was clear, she slowly got to her feet, straightened her rumpled purple dress, hitched a pack similar to Ellen's over one shoulder, and made her way to where Ellen and Merry waited.

After giving Ellen a quick hug, she turned to Merry and gave a strangled gasp. She stepped forward to push the wrap off Merry's head and placed a hand on her cheek, wonder in her eyes.

Then she frowned and dropped her hand. 'You are not Meredith Meadows,' she said in a whisper.

Merry shook her head but said nothing. Now was not the time to explain exactly who she was.

Ellen tugged on Debra's arm and they set off through the trees, Benny and Sadie running along beside them, moving as quickly as they could given the need to not be heard. After a few steps Debra lowered her hand and the rat launched himself from a bush and climbed up to her shoulder as they went.

Merry had no idea where Ellen was headed now, sure they could not return to the cottage, but all she cared about at that moment was putting as much distance as possible between themselves and the guild camp.

Gabriel had intended to meet up with this group in the morning, and dawn's soft light was rapidly brightening. He and the others couldn't be far away.

They had to get out of there before he and the other enforcers arrived, or the ones that had arrested Debra woke up and realised she was gone. Even as the thought formed in her head, a shout rose behind them.

'Run,' called Ellen in a low voice, suiting her actions to her cry.

Merry picked up the hem of her dress, stepping over tree roots and fallen branches as quickly as she could. It was getting lighter, making it easier to see obstacles in their path, but meaning it would be easier for their pursuers to spot them too. Up ahead, Ellen and Debra dodged around a large tree. Merry went around the other side, and then cursed as her feet slipped in wet leaves. She flung out an arm and grabbed hold of the tree to right herself and then kept going. She could hear the sound of her friends ahead but could no longer see them. She continued, relying on the sound of their passage to keep her on their trail.

Soon even that sound faded and Merry stopped, panic filling her at the realisation she had lost them. In her mind, she called out to Sadie, hoping the little cat would hear her, but got no response.

A shout came from behind her, a man's voice, and Merry took off in the other direction. She would not let them catch her. Branches whipped against her as she ran, uncaring of the direction, just wanting to get away. She skirted a large tree, once again slipping on the wet leaves, and then froze.

On the other side of the tree stood Gabriel Fair-weather.

Shock wreathed his features at the sight of her, but then determination replaced it.

Merry turned to run away, but wind whipped around her, buffeting her in place even as goose bumps rippled across her entire body. No matter which way she turned, the wind pushed her back.

Gasping, shaking, she turned to face Gabriel once more.

The wind stopped pushing at her as Gabriel moved forward.

Merry scrambled backward. 'Don't come any closer.' She held out a hand to ward him off, not that it would do any good when he had the power to immobilise her with wind.

Her heel caught on a fallen tree branch and she flailed her arms to aid her balance. Gabriel lunged forward and she gave a strangled scream. But all he did was latch onto her hand, holding her upright.

'I don't want to hurt you,' he said, gazing intently at her. 'Won't you tell me your name?'

She opened her mouth and he gave her hand a squeeze. 'Your real name,' he said with a smile. 'Please?'

With a sigh, she said, 'Merry.'

His smile widened. 'Thank you, Merry.'

When he said her name her hand tingled where he

still held it, warmth spreading up her arm, and she pulled against his grip.

Gabriel released her hand and took a step back. 'I'm sorry I frightened you, Merry. Please, don't run away. I just want to talk to you.'

He seemed sincere but as she rubbed her hand and her fingers grazed the bruising on her wrist from where she had been bound, she scowled. 'If talk was all you wanted why did you get your enforcer to tie me up?'

He winced. 'I'm afraid Kassandra was overzealous. She thinks you're a threat. That you are a danger to the guild.'

'I don't want anything to do with the guild. This is all a mistake. I shouldn't even be here. I wish you people would leave me alone.' Her voice rose with each statement, and she bit her bottom lip to keep from saying more. She had to get a grip. She could not lose it in front of this guy.

'I'm afraid we can't do that. Not yet. But I promise we mean you no harm.' He gave her a sympathetic smile as he lowered his hands. 'I realise this must be upsetting, but all we want to do is talk to you, to figure out why you look so much like a mage who tried to destroy the guild in the past.'

Merry stifled a grimace. 'Why does it matter what I look like? I'm not her. Please, just let me go.'

He sighed. 'I wish I could. But now the enforcers are aware of your existence, they will continue to pursue you until they are assured you are no longer a threat.

But it doesn't have to be like that. Come with me, to the guild tower, and once you have met with my aunt, Ophelia Fairweather, and answered a few questions, you will be free to go on with your life.'

Merry frowned. 'I already told you, I'm not supposed to be here. No amount of questions will change the fact I accidentally triggered a spell that brought me to Tirana. All I want to do is go home.' She had to get through to him. Get him to see she wasn't the enemy.

*She must be from the old world. That would explain why she is reluctant to accompany you to the guild tower. But not why she looks almost exactly like Meredith Meadow did as a young woman. Ask her what her bloodline is. Maybe she is a throwback.*

Merry looked around and saw the grey and white cat from the night before perched on the branch of a tree behind Gabriel, its coat shining silver in the sun's light.

'I am not a throwback.' Merry glared at the cat.

Gabriel gaped at her. 'You heard Beethoven?'

Too late, Merry remembered what Ellen had said, about only powerful magic users being able to hear the mental voices of familiars other than their own.

She lifted her chin. 'What if I did? It doesn't mean anything. This is not my world. All I want to do is fix the spell that brought me here so I can go home. I don't have time to go to the guild tower to meet your aunt.'

'My aunt is a very powerful mage. She could help you fix the transportation spell. If you come with me willingly, I will ensure you are well looked after. If you resist, the enforcers will make the journey far less pleasant, and it would distress me to see you hurt.'

The entreaty in his voice tugged at Merry, and he did look sincere. Still, when his aunt found out she was Meredith Meadows' granddaughter, her sworn enemy, she was sure the last thing she would want to do would be to help Merry.

A shout rose in the distance and Gabriel turned his head to look in the direction it had come from. Then he faced Merry again, holding out a hand. 'Please, come with me and you have my vow that no harm will come to you.'

*You better hope she doesn't hold you to that.* The familiar, Beethoven, jumped down from the branch, and landed lightly beside Gabriel. *You may be able to bend these enforcers to your will, but you're not strong enough to go up against your aunt.*

Gabriel shot the cat a disgruntled glare. 'It will be fine. My aunt is an honourable woman. She will help Merry get home, I'm sure of it.'

*A witch who can hear familiars? Not even you are that naive, Gabriel.*

Merry twitched at the cat's words. 'Is he right? Will your aunt try to make me join the guild, whether I want to or not?' That was what Ellen had said would happen.

Gabriel grimaced. 'My aunt only wants what is best for all Tirana. In the past, magic users have been taken advantage of by the crown. She formed the guild to protect them.'

'Wanting to protect people is one thing. Forcing them to join the guild whether they want to or not is another,' said Merry.

'As you are not from here, I am sure she would not enforce guild law in this instance.'

'How sure?'

'What?'

Merry gave a snort and crossed her arms in front of her chest. 'You keep saying you are sure your aunt would help me. How sure are you, that what you are saying is the truth?'

Gabriel stiffened, his expression troubled.

Merry sighed, sure she had her answer. 'Look, if you really wanted to help me you would turn around and forget you even saw me.'

'You would have me lie to the enforcers, to my aunt?'

'Yes.'

More shouts came from behind Gabriel, louder, closer. The enforcers would soon stumble upon them. Merry had to convince him to let her go before that happened.

She took a deep breath. 'If there is any doubt in you, about what your aunt might do if I were to go to the guild tower with you, then you should let me go now. Or the vow you just gave me is worthless.'

Indecision flitted over his face.

*Told you so.*

'Beethoven, be quiet,' said Gabriel, frustration lacing his words as he faced Merry. 'My vow was to see no harm come to you if you chose to willingly accompany me to the tower. That vow still stands.'

Merry narrowed her eyes. 'You would go up against your aunt, even though you are no match for her, if she tries to harm me?'

His gaze was steady. 'Yes.'

Again, Merry wavered. His aunt was a powerful mage, maybe the most powerful one in Tirana. She should easily be able to fix the spell… a spell that was inside the spell box that was in Ellen's pack. Not that not having it should be a problem. If her grandmother had been able to make it from scratch, surely Ophelia Fair-weather would be able to make another one. But the guild leader considered her grandmother to be a sworn enemy. Would that enmity transfer to her grand-daughter?

Merry couldn't risk it. She had to get away.

She cast around her, looking for something she could use to distract Gabriel long enough for her to escape, something to stop him using his magic to subdue her. All she saw was grass and leaves. And the branch she had almost tripped over.

With a deep breath, she reached up and undid the wrap from around her head, loosening the bun and allowing her hair to fall down around her shoulders. Gabriel's eyes widened and he stepped forward to touch a lock of hair that curled around her neck and down the front of her arm.

'What a remarkable colour,' he said, running his fingers through the lock of hair.

'Don't touch me,' said Merry, pulling away even as she bent down and scooped up the branch.

'I apologise. I don't know what came—'

Bang. The end of the branch hit him on the side of the head. He reeled, stumbling backward, the hand that had been touching her hair going to where she had hit him.

She swung the branch again.

*Look out.*

The cat's warning came a split second before Merry rammed the end of the branch into Gabriel's stomach. Air whooshed out of his lungs and he doubled over. Beethoven hissed and ran at Merry and she swung the branch to scare the cat off, not wanting to hurt him. She hadn't wanted to hurt Gabriel either, but she could not let herself be recaptured.

As Gabriel fought to regain his breath, she turned and ran, jumping small bushes and fallen branches as she went, unheeding of what direction she was going in. All she wanted to do was get as far away from Gabriel as she could so he wouldn't be able to use his magic on her.

A long time later, her own lungs gasping for air and a stitch in her side, she slowed her pace. There were no sounds of pursuit behind her, but she couldn't risk stopping. She wound her way through trees and bushes, calling out to Sadie in her mind, hoping the little cat would be able to hear her. She was lost in the middle of a forest in a foreign land, with no food or water, and an unknown number of people chasing her.

As much as Tirana might appear to be the same as back home, though far more rustic and with magic, she had no idea what kinds of predators might live in this forest, or what plants were safe to eat. She had no wilderness skills, nothing that could help her survive. As she walked, Merry gripped the branch she'd clobbered Gabriel with. She felt bad about having hit him, but there'd been no alternative. As she thought of the thud it had made as it collided with the side of his head, her guilt worsened. She hoped he was okay.

Maybe one of the enforcers was capable of healing. Ellen had said some magic users were able to harness more than one form of magic. Enforcers could manipulate objects, and people, with their minds, but that did not mean they had no other skills. For all Merry knew, Gabriel would be able to heal himself. If he had only a minor ability, it probably wouldn't be displayed like his affinity for Air and Water.

She had no idea what he could do with his Water magic, but he had already demonstrated his Air magic in the wind that had stopped her from running away from him earlier. Still, she wished she hadn't had to hit him, twice, to get away. She was not a violent person. She much preferred to make things than to destroy them.

She ran her hands along the length of the wood, distracting herself from her guilt and current predicament by thinking what she could make with it. It was long and straight, and felt solid in her hands. She mainly worked with silver and small gems but had sometimes carved small pieces of wood into pendants and earrings to sell in *Bling and Baubles*. For a branch that was so straight and of a good length, it would be better made into something like a staff.

Mages used staffs, right? At least the ones she had read about and seen in movies did. Maybe she could work with it, carve a design into the wood and make a staff out of it. Then, before she left Tirana, she could see about finding a way to get it to Gabriel, as a peace offering of sorts.

She gave a snort. He was sure to love being gifted with the branch she had clobbered him with.

Despite her doubts about how such a gift would be received, the creative urge helped calm her scattered thoughts as she walked. The branch warmed beneath her hands as she imagined it scraped clean of bark and with a pattern carved into it. Considering Gabriel had used wind against her, maybe she would carve lines to represent the movement of air. Not clouds, but a swirling pattern that would make it seem as if the staff itself was moving in the breeze, like the pendant Gabriel wore.

As she walked, running her hands up and down the branch that might one day become a staff, she scanned her surroundings, hoping to find something that looked familiar.

There.

Was that the tree they had sheltered beneath during the storm?

Merry hurried closer and peered into the hollow, a feeling of accomplishment sweeping through her when she saw the discarded lantern. Yes, it was the same tree. She stood with her back to the hollow and tried to pinpoint where they had come from, when they'd left the cottage in search of Ellen's mentor. Not that she wanted to retrace their steps. She also didn't want to go in the direction they had taken to get to the enforcers' camp. But at least she kind of knew where she was.

Now to find the others.

She scanned the trees around her, gripping the branch tightly in her hands as she tried to decide which direction she should take. Where had the others fled to, after they'd freed Ellen's mentor?

A shiver swept over her as she angled herself to the left of the path they had taken to get to the enforcers' camp, still running her hands over the branch in a motion that helped calm and centre her. She felt the urge to start walking, sure she would find her friends if she chose this direction.

She resisted the urge as she considered her other options. Behind her was where she had encountered Gabriel. If she went left, she would find herself back at the cottage, while the right would lead straight to the enforcers' camp. Decision made for her, she set off in the direction she was facing, hoping she was going the right way. Every now and then she would call out to

Sadie in her mind, the words echoing in her head with no reply.

Hunger gnawed at her, and her mouth was so dry she contemplated seeing if there was any raindrops left on the leaves of the trees. Even though the sun had fully risen, the branches towering above her shielded a lot of the light, but each leaf she checked was as dry as her mouth. Her feet ached, leg muscles straining, but she kept going. Surely, even if she didn't find the others, she would eventually reach the end of the forest and be able to see something other than trees.

When the muscles in her legs began to ache even more, Merry realised the ground was rising. She looked ahead and could see what appeared to be a grey stone wall that was taller than she was, the trees thinning the closer she got to it. She sped up, hope giving her aching body fresh strength at this sign of habitation. A wall had to mean people, who might give her food and water.

As she drew closer, she saw the wall was crumbling. It looked old, weathered and on the verge of collapse, as if a strong wind would knock it down. Struggling to hold on to her optimism, Merry stepped closer. She hit something, an invisible barrier, and gasped as a shiver swept over her entire body. The branch in her hands grew uncomfortably warm and the hair on her arms stood on end. Then, as quickly as the sensation started it was over and she was near enough to touch the crumbling stone wall if she wished. Not that she wanted to risk it.

She walked down the length of the wall until she found a section that had crumbled inward, and carefully manoeuvred herself through the gap. Her confidence received a boost at seeing a number of low brick buildings with cobbled paths between them a short distance away. As she grew closer her initial hopefulness faded. The paths were liberally sprinkled with weeds and the cottages appeared to be in as bad a shape as the wall. The sense she was being watched rose, but there was no sound, no sign this place was inhabited.

The place had an eerie air to it that had Merry checking over her shoulder every five seconds. She wanted to get as far away from it as possible and doubted she would find anything there to help her survive or to reconnect with her friends. But at the very least, this was somewhere to hide out if the enforcers found her again. There were buildings of various sizes, some looking to be homes while others were large enough to be communal areas. She poked her head through windows as she went and found most of them contained rotting wooden furniture. There was no sign of other furnishings or belongings of those who had once lived here. The feeling of being watched remained, and yet each time she glanced behind her she was always alone. There was not even the sound of birds to be heard, making her feel as though she was in some kind of bubble, shut away from the rest of the world.

She continued through to the other side of what may have once been a thriving community and broke through the line of buildings to find the ruins of a gateway in the section of wall on this side, only the metal hinges remaining intact. She poked her head out through the opening to find more untamed forest. Here she could once again hear birds chirping in the trees, but there was no sign of her friends or even the enforcers and Gabriel.

She returned to the buildings, still hoping she would find something, anything, to help her.

An hour later, growing even more dejected with the results of her search, Merry was inside one of the larger buildings, checking out the rooms contained within, when she heard voices. She slipped to a window with a rotted timber frame to peer out, sure it had to be Gabriel and the enforcers. Relief swept through her at the sight of Ellen, with her arms around the woman they'd rescued that morning. In front of them walked Sadie, tail high, ears alert, while Benny was perched on Ellen's shoulder. As Merry watched, Sadie's head swivelled in her direction.

Merry waved and called out, 'I am so glad to see you guys.'

Ellen's eyes went wide when she spotted Merry, and then a relieved smile appeared on her face. 'Merry, you're okay. We were so worried.'

Merry dropped the branch she had been carrying since clobbering Gabriel on the floor below the window. Then she darted to the doorway of the building and ran outside, joining her friends.

Sadie wound around her legs, giving a soft meow. *I knew you would find your way here. It is in your blood.*

Merry gave the cat a quick pat and then made her way to the other side of Ellen's mentor and slipped her arm over her shoulder. The poor woman's face was pinched with pain, her body shook, and she was holding one foot off the ground as she attempted to hobble along. Ellen steered them in the direction of the building Merry had just left.

'We were going to come back for you, I swear,' said Ellen, casting a stricken look Merry's way as they lowered her mentor to the stone floor once they were inside. 'I just needed to get Debra somewhere safe first.'

'It's okay,' said Merry, shaking her head. 'I was fine.' Well, not exactly fine, but she had survived, whereas Debra looked to be in far worse condition than when she had escaped from the enforcers' camp.

'What happened?' Merry asked.

'She tripped over an exposed root and broke her ankle,' said Ellen as she helped ease her mentor into a more comfortable position.

Benny jumped from Ellen's shoulder and curled into the crook of Debra's neck, watching intently as the young healer rummaged in her herb satchel. She selected a few samples before pulling out one of the timber mugs and filling it from the water skin she had filled at the creek the day before.

Goose bumps swept over Merry's arms as Ellen

closed her eyes, lips moving in a silent spell, and held a hand over the mug.

'Hold her up,' said Ellen once she was done.

Benny scooted aside as Merry wrapped an arm around Debra's back, propping her up while Ellen held the mug to her lips.

'This will help with the pain while I bind your ankle,' said Ellen.

Debra sipped at the mug, some of the tightness easing in her face, though she winced as Ellen began to work on the ankle. Benny settled on her lap and she stroked his head as she eyed Merry, who was still supporting her.

'So,' she said in a strained voice, 'you are Meredith's granddaughter. Ellen tells me she has passed on.' Sadness wreathed her features. 'I was sorry to hear that. She and I were good friends in our youth, as was Ophelia Fairweather, to both of us, before the choices Ophelia made in regard to the guild tore us apart. I heard Meredith had been imprisoned by the guild and was on my way with a group of those who opposed Ophelia's new laws to try to free her when word came that she had escaped to the old world, and that gave me hope we would one day meet again.'

'I'm sorry,' said Merry. 'I never met her. My father never forgave her for returning here and abandoning him.'

'That is indeed sad news,' said Debra, reaching out to

pat Merry's hand. 'But you are here in her stead, so perhaps all is not lost.'

Merry frowned. 'What do you mean?'

'Ellen tells me you have the makings of a powerful mage,' said Debra. 'You hear the voice of more than your own familiar. With training, you will be as powerful a mage as your grandmother. Powerful enough to break the hold the guild has on our brethren.'

Merry shook her head. 'I don't want to be a mage, and I have no intention of breaking anything. I just want to go home.'

'Not a mage? Then how did you come by that?' Debra pointed to where Merry had placed the branch she'd whacked Gabriel with. Only, it wasn't a simple branch anymore.

Its lines were smooth, the bark gone, and in its place was a pale wood with an intricate pattern carved in it; a pattern like the one she had imagined as she walked, one that was meant to represent the flow of the wind.

Merry's mouth hung open, and she scanned the rest of the space, sure it couldn't be her branch. But there was no other in sight, and that was where she had left hers.

'And how did you enter Ralinin, if you do not possess the capability to wield Spirit magic? The barrier would have kept you from stepping past the wall, even as dilapidated as it is. Magic is steeped into the very ground here, making it almost impossible for those without Spirit magic in their blood to set foot inside the ruins.'

Head shaking, Merry fought to deny Debra's words. But she remembered the feeling as she'd drawn close to the wall, the sensation of being impeded at first. Then there was the way the branch had turned into a staff. Thinking back, she remembered it had warmed in her hands, both as she walked and when she'd entered the town.

Was it possible? Did she have the potential to become a powerful mage?

The thought of being able to wield magic both terrified and excited her. But if she was able to get the spell fixed and return home, whether she could do magic or not would no longer matter. Sadie had said magic was limited in her world, except for certain places, like near the portal. She would go back to being Merry Meadows, unemployed and broke, at least until she sold her grandmother's bookshop.

*If* she sold it.

The bookshop housed the portal to Tirana. Like her grandmother, she would not have to give up magic entirely if she were to remain in Belwich, living in the tiny residence above *Merry Magic*. She pictured herself running the shop, making jewellery she could sell alongside the books and learning to use magic. She had never pictured herself living in such a tiny town, but a glance at the branch she had somehow turned into a staff made her wonder what else she could make with magic.

For the first time she began to think that coming to Tirana may not have been a disaster.

Merry itched to ask Debra about fixing the spell but forced herself to wait until Ellen had finished wrapping her mentor's broken ankle and made her as comfortable as she could in the old building. As she worked, Ellen kept stopping, clasping a hand on her chest and the other over Debra's leg, murmuring her silent spell.

Goose bumps swept over Merry each time she did it, as when Ellen had treated the water the day before. She'd had goose bumps when Gabriel used wind to keep her from running away when she'd encountered him in the forest as well, but she was starting to think it wasn't from being cold.

'Can other people sense when you are using magic?' The question blurted out of Merry. She eyed the staff again. She hadn't felt a shiver as she'd held it, but it had warmed beneath her hands.

It was Debra who answered her. 'Yes, though most witches or mages are more sensitive to when someone is using one of the magic elements they also wield.' Her eyes narrowed as she surveyed Merry. 'You can sense Ellen's magic.'

'I think so, maybe.' Merry rubbed her arms. 'At least, I got goose bumps when Ellen treated creek water to make it safe to drink and to give us energy, and while she is healing you. I got them with Gabriel too, when he used wind to stop me getting away from him.'

'You saw Gabriel Fairweather again?' Ellen's eyes were wide when she twisted around to look at Merry.

Merry filled her in on the encounter, and then said, 'I felt bad about hitting him, but I had to get away. I took off as fast as I could and didn't stop until I found this place.'

Debra nodded. 'You did what you had to do, and if you are anything like your grandmother you will have an affinity for all five magical elements.'

Ellen gasped, her hands falling away from Debra's leg. 'I knew you would make a powerful mage, but to have five elements under your control...' She shook her head.

Merry grimaced. 'I can't control anything.'

'Yet,' said Debra. 'With time and training you could be a mage powerful enough to rival Ophelia Fairweather.'

'Gabriel said his aunt would help me, that all she

would want to do was ask questions. But his familiar said she would never let me go.'

Debra nodded again. 'You are a threat. Even untrained. She could not risk you joining those who rebel against her rules. She would make you swear an oath to the guild, binding your powers for her use. She will not stop until either you join her, or you are dead.'

The faint hope that Beethoven had been wrong, and Gabriel would be able to safeguard her with his vow, died. Merry had to get home before she wound up as a prisoner in the guild tower, stuck in Tirana forever.

She looked to Debra. 'My grandmother's spell, the one in the spell box that brought me here. It's broken. Ellen said you might be able to fix it.'

Ellen reached into her bag and pulled it out, handing it to Debra.

A look of wonder tinged Debra's face when she opened the spell box and surveyed the contents. She gave a sigh as she handed the box to Merry. 'Meredith was an artist. Her spells were as beautiful as they were powerful.'

The jumble of items in the box, two gems, some silver wire, a shell and what appeared to be the fossil of a tiny winged creature, didn't look beautiful at the moment, though Merry knew the objects could be transformed into art by a talented artist. She had often used objects she found in her jewellery, when the shape of them inspired a design. From the way the wire in the spell box was shaped, and gaps in the design, she thought it had once been a brooch.

She would easily be able to reshape the items in the box back into a brooch, if that was all it took. To imbue the brooch with magic was another story.

'Can you fix it?' she asked.

Debra gave a sigh. 'A spell to split the veil between this world and the one you come from requires charms from all five magic elements, Air, Water, Fire, Earth and Spirit. I am a Spirit mage, with an affinity for Water and Air, but I do not have any affinity for Fire or Earth.'

She wore a chagrined expression as she waved a hand at her broken ankle. 'The ability to heal comes from the Earth, which would be extremely useful to me right now, to assist Ellen in healing. But it is not so.'

Ellen hung her head. 'I wish I could do more, but I'm not strong enough.'

Debra reached out and laid a hand on Ellen's arm. 'You have done more than enough. If not for you, I would still be a captive of the enforcers, on my way to the tower to face Ophelia's judgement.'

'Merry helped too,' said Ellen, 'and Benny and Sadie.'

Debra wore a fond expression as she gave the rat sleeping in her lap a pat, and then looked to where Sadie sat near the door, looking out. 'Benny has been a faithful companion, and it is wonderful to see Sadie again, though sad that Meredith is not with her.'

She turned to Merry. 'Though I am sure she will be

just as faithful a companion to you, and I thank you both for your assistance in my rescue.'

Merry didn't think she did much other than communicate with the rat. But she gave Debra a small smile.

Then, determined to get the conversation back on track, she said, 'There must be some way to fix the spell. I need to get home before the end of the month or *Huntington Inc.* will withdraw their offer to buy the bookshop.' Not that she was sure she wanted to sell it. But it would be nice to have the option.

'Huntington?'

*Huntington.*

Merry looked from Debra to Sadie. Both of them stared back at her with wide eyes. 'You've heard of them?'

'Bartholomew Huntington was the name of the man who led the most vicious band of witch hunters to ever walk the Earth. It is because of him that our ancestors were forced to flee to Tirana,' said Debra.

*If this company has ties with the witch hunters, it is dire news indeed that they wish to purchase* Merry Magic. Sadie's eyes narrowed and her tail twitched.

Merry's mouth was dry as she said, 'The day my grandmother died, *Huntington Inc.* bought the shopping complex where I worked. They found a legal loophole to allow them to terminate the leases and evict all the businesses who had shops there, meaning I lost my job. The same thing happened with the flat I rented, although I was never told who bought it. Only that I had until the end of the month to find a new place.' All these events had Merry in need of money fast, which might have made her less likely to baulk at selling the bookshop.

'But the witch hunts took place hundreds of years ago. How could a company who wants to buy a book-shop be related to witch hunters?' Even as she said it, dread settled in her stomach. 'The portal.'

Debra's face paled. 'If witch hunters are still active in your world, gaining access to a portal would allow them to come here and continue their campaign to eradicate all those who possess magic.'

Merry waved a hand at the broken contents of the spell box. 'Wouldn't they need a spell to open the portal, and someone with magic to use it?'

Expression grim, Debra said, 'In the past, they used torture to subvert witches to their cause. Once their will was broken, these poor wretches were forced to ply their magic at the will of the hunter who had command of them and to help capture or kill more of our brethren. Dark would be the day witch hunters gain access to Tirana.'

*Magic may be weaker in your world, but it was not unknown. Therefore, Meredith kept strong wards on the book-shop to prevent those with ill intentions from setting foot within the shop. They would have to be specifically invited to cross the threshold to gain access.*

Merry swallowed heavily at Sadie's words, remember-ing how Mr Creepy had asked her to invite him inside *Merry Magic* so he could go over the contract with her. What if she'd said yes? The witch hunters would already have access to the portal.

'Are the wards strong enough to keep witch hunters out, and other witches if they have any working for them?' Merry hoped the answer was yes. She did not like the idea of hunters appearing in Tirana and going after Ellen simply because she could do magic. She no longer believed it was a coincidence that so much had gone wrong in her life in the past two weeks. *Huntington Inc.* had to be after the portal.

*The wards weaken over time. Meredith performed a spell to renew them four times a year, at the beginning of each season. We need to return to your world as soon as possible, and I will instruct you in the spell to renew the wards. It is the only way to protect Tirana.*

Merry relayed Sadie's words to Debra, finishing with, 'We need to find someone who can remake the spell so Sadie and I can go home and renew the wards.' She hoped the spell to do so would not be difficult. Unconsciously turning a branch into a staff was one thing. Working a real spell was another.

Debra shook her head. 'It cannot be remade. And even if I did have the power of all five elements, the spell would not work for you. It must be keyed to the blood of the maker, and only one of my bloodline would be able to use it. But fear not, my dear, there is still a way for you to get home. You can make a new spell.'

'Me?'

'You have the potential to master all five elements,

as your grandmother did. Magic is a part of you, a part that is already beginning to materialise. The longer you remain in Tirana, the stronger your magic will become. You must learn to control it, or risk it running wild and creating irreparable damage, to yourself and others.'

Goose bumps swept over Merry that had nothing to do with sensing magic. Was it true? Was she a danger to herself and others?

'I don't know the first thing about magic, and I don't have time to learn anything other than how to renew wards. If the witch hunters really are trying to get here, we have to stop them. And you said the guild will never stop looking for me. I need to get home before they find me. For all I know, they are on their way here, now, to capture all of us.'

With a sad look, Debra shook her head. 'They will not come here. This place is cursed.'

'What?'

'Ralinin was once a thriving community, where witches and mages with an affinity for Spirit came to learn how to master their powers. When Ophelia formed the guild to protect us from being abused by the crown, many of us joined her. But when the war was over, and we wished to return to our homes, she sought to stop us. She insisted we must remain part of the guild, to stop the crown, or anyone else, from trying to control us. Some stayed, but many, your grandmother and I among them, did not wish to have anything more to do with war. We refused to swear an oath to the guild and returned here.'

Tears glistened in her eyes as she recounted her story. 'When word came that Ophelia was using threats to force mages to join the guild, we knew it would not be long before she turned her eyes back to us. But still we were not prepared when an army of enforcers arrived at the gates and demanded entry. They brought with them a powerful Spirit mage, to take our oaths and make them binding. We refused and the enforcers forced their way through the gates, seeking to subdue us. We fought back, and many died that day. Those with Spirit magic who fought with us and were mortally wounded used their very essence to turn the enforcers away, cursing the land. No enforcer has been able to set foot within the gates ever since, and those who do not have an affinity with Spirit are tormented if they somehow make it past the wall.'

Merry cast a wary glance at the shadows in the room, wondering if the sense of being watched that she'd had since setting foot in the ruins had been the eyes of those who had died here, preparing to unleash their curse on her. She gulped down fear at the thought.

Debra looked to Ellen. 'I'm sorry my dear, but you will not be able to remain here much longer. I am holding them back, but once I sleep you will be unprotected.'

Ellen nodded. 'I know. But you will be safe here.'

'Before you leave, I will try to determine Merry's

path,' said Debra. 'Your actions will have set the guild against you as well. They know you travel with Merry, and you will both be in danger once you venture from here. You must help her and Sadie get back to the old world, to prevent witch hunters from gaining access to Tirana. Please, hand me my pack.'

Ellen grabbed the bag and handed it to Debra, who reached inside and pulled out a small silk bag with a drawstring. Careful not to dislodge the sleeping rat, she opened it up and pulled out a pack of cards. The backs were a beautiful shimmering purple with a gold pentacle embossed in the centre.

Merry gasped when Debra began to shuffle the cards and she spotted the colourful images on the front of them. 'They're Tarot cards.'

'Yes, Merry, and with these we shall find your path.' She handed the deck to Merry and got her to shuffle them. Then she took them back and leaned to the side to lay out a pattern on the stone floor.

Merry scanned the cards, unable to discern the meaning as one by one Debra turned them over.

'This layout represents your journey. It deals with the control of your ability and accessing your powers. It signifies the five magical elements you must master to create the charms needed for the spell to return you home. You must travel to the focal point for each of the elemental leylines, and there you will be tasked with a challenge. Succeed and you will receive what you need. Fail, and the guild will take you.' Her expression grew grim as she looked up at Merry. 'If this happens, a great evil will descend on Tirana.'

Merry stiffened as Debra spoke. 'The witch hunters?'

'What form the evil will take is shrouded, but I fear so.'

'How am I expected to master five elements?' Merry couldn't imagine it would be an easy process.

'True mastery takes years. What this journey signifies is your willingness to open yourself up, to allow the magical spark inside you to flare to life. Only then will you be able to make the transportation spell. But you will not travel alone. Ellen will be with you, and she can help you learn to access your powers.'

Ellen gasped. 'I can't be a teacher. I can barely do anything.'

Debra smiled at her. 'You are stronger than you think. It is your strength of character, the conviction of your beliefs, that Merry needs. I am not expecting you to show her how to wield a fireball or conjure a storm. Guide her to find that spark inside her, so she can fully connect with her true self, and the rest will come.'

Merry didn't blame Ellen for appearing daunted by the task Debra had set her. She was terrified by the thought of becoming a mage, working to control elements she knew nothing about. Sure, she had heard about them, but that was different from trying to control them. But she had to. If she wanted to go home. The alternative would be to give up and hand herself over to the guild, and then wait for the witch hunters to come pouring through the portal and destroy them all.

'It will not be an easy journey, but if you take this path, you will be rewarded tenfold,' said Debra.

Merry stifled a grimace. She didn't want rewards. She just wanted to go home, and for her new friends to not be in danger.

'Where will this journey take us?' Ellen asked, her voice shaking slightly as she clutched at her chest.

Debra propped herself up, wincing as she did so, and then grabbed a twig to scratch out a rudimentary map in the stone floor. 'Tirana is crossed with leylines, with focal points in the north, south, east and west for Air, Earth, Water and Fire, while Tirana's Spirit resides in the heart.' She tapped her twig in the centre of her drawing.

'That's the guild tower,' said Ellen. 'We have to go there?'

'Yes. But you must travel to each of the other focal points first, so Merry can find suitable charms. Once she has all four, then you will have to make your way to the tower and the Spirit focal point below it to find one last charm. It will not be easy, to get there without being caught, but it is the only way to get Merry home.'

'Then what?' Merry asked, looking from Debra to Ellen.

'Benny and I will meet you there, once my ankle is healed enough for me to travel. Then we will find a way to get you to where you need to be to work the transportation spell. Once you have returned to the old world, Sadie will be able to instruct you in how to harness what you have learned from your journey to access the elements needed to renew Meredith's wards.'

Merry hoped it worked out that way, but she had a feeling it was going to be far more difficult than Debra made it sound.

Debra packed away her cards and lay back on the makeshift pillow Ellen made for her, eyes closing. 'I can't sleep, not until the two of you are clear,' she said, weariness in her voice.

A loud bang came from outside, making Benny spring up from Debra's lap to her shoulder. *The spirits are growing increasingly restless, Debra. It is time for you to say your goodbyes.*

A shadow flickered at the corner of Merry's eye and she spun. She could see nothing, just as when she had entered the ruined town, but she sensed eyes on her, and movement beyond the building.

'The spirits are angry,' said Debra, her voice even fainter than before. 'They sense the enforcers in the forest beyond, just outside the wall. The enforcers have guessed this is where we are hiding but are too afraid to enter. Wisely so. The spirits would tear them to pieces. Kassandra Piermont's father was one of those who led the attack. I am not sure how much longer I can hold them back.' Debra opened her eyes and looked to Ellen. 'You must leave now.'

'You're not in a condition to take care of yourself,'

said Ellen, worry throbbing in her voice. 'I can't leave you.'

'You must. If you stay here much longer, the spirits' anger will be uncontrollable. They are my brethren. Once I am alone, they will settle and will assist me as I heal. You must leave me. It is for the best.'

From the thrashing sounds and bangs and ghastly moans coming from outside, Merry was all too ready to leave. Yet to do so would be to hand themselves over to the enforcers. 'How are we supposed to get out of here if the place is surrounded?'

'There is a tunnel we sent the elderly and the very young through, during the attack.' Debra lifted a hand and beckoned to Merry. 'Come closer, and I will show you where it is.'

Merry leaned over and Debra placed a hand on her forehead. Instantly a series of images played in Merry's head, showing the way the place had once been, filled with life. It showed her the tunnel that some had used to escape while the others fought to give them time to get away. Then a new series of images played, showing the ruins as they were now, a light illuminating the way to the tunnel entrance.

Debra's hand fell away, and Merry gasped as her normal sight returned. Then she wished it hadn't.

A ghostly spectre hovered through the doorway, streaking towards Ellen.

Without thinking, she picked up her staff and swung

it at the spectre. It howled, chill air filling the space as it was pushed backward.

'Hurry,' gasped out Debra. 'Merry, you would never have been able to enter Ralinin alone if you did not have an affinity for Spirit. You must protect Ellen.' Then her eyes rolled back in her head and she went still.

'No.' Ellen launched to her mentor's side, hands grasping her neck. She sagged. 'She's alive, just unconscious.'

She looked up at Merry. 'I can't leave her.'

*We need to leave, before it is too late.* Sadie bounded in front of Merry, tail twitching, ears flicking, as the noise outside intensified.

More howls came and a fierce chill wind swept through the room. Merry could see through more spectres gathering beyond the doorway. Without Debra's protection, they were preparing to assault Ellen. Sadie was right, they had to go now or lose the chance forever.

She stood, holding the staff in front of her with one hand. 'We have to go now. They're mad. They'll kill you.'

Ellen rifled in her pack, pulling out the food she had gathered at Debra's ransacked cottage and the water canteen, piling it all on the ground beside her unconscious mentor. Then, after one last despairing look at Debra, Ellen gave a nod. She straightened her shoulders and stepped closer to Merry. 'Get us out of here.'

Barely able to believe what she was doing, Merry grabbed hold of Ellen's arm and together they stepped into the courtyard to face the ghosts of the dead. They had died to protect this place and even in death that urge remained. Not releasing her grip on Ellen, she swung the staff in the air in front of her, relieved when the closest spectres backed off. As quickly as she dared, Merry used the images Debra had projected into her head to guide her to the entrance to the tunnel that would lead them to safety.

She hoped.

What if the enforcers knew about the escape route?

Either way, they couldn't stay here. The spectres' anger was palpable, thickening the air around them and making it hard to walk upright. Sadie slunk along low to the ground, fur ruffled by the wind created by the spectres' movements. Pressure built up in Merry's head and pain flared in the hand holding Ellen's arm, but she resisted the urge to let go. They wanted her to abandon her friend, so they could set upon her at will.

No. She would not let that happen.

Merry gritted her teeth and concentrated on putting one foot in front of the other, even as she willed her staff to push back the spectres. Beside her she could hear Ellen whimpering, but she had no time to spare to comfort her. They had to get out of there.

Step by step they made it to the edge of the building that contained the tunnel entrance, but Merry knew they were not free yet. She checked Sadie was still close on her heels as she and Ellen ran for the doorway. As if sensing they were about to lose their prey, the spectres redoubled their efforts, blocking the way.

Merry roared as she swung the staff, imagining a fierce wind sweeping the spirits away. Warmth flared through her body and travelled into the staff. A strong wind sprang up, sweeping aside the spectres and clearing the doorway. Not stopping to think about what she had done, Merry pushed Ellen ahead of her and into the exposed tunnel. Sadie streaked ahead of them as Merry slid her hand down Ellen's arm to grasp her hand and the two of them ran as fast as they could after the little black cat, into the dark tunnel, not stopping until the ghastly moans of the spectres had faded in the distance.

Ellen stumbled, her hand falling from Merry's grip as she fell. Merry felt around in the dark until she found her friend hunched over on the floor of the tunnel, head bowed, sobs racking her body.

'I shouldn't have left her. She needed me.'

Merry knelt and wrapped her free arm around Ellen's shoulders, wishing it wasn't dark. They would both feel much better if they could see where they were.

To her surprise, her staff began to glow, illuminating the space around them enough for her to see her friend's face and the shine of Sadie's eyes a short distance away.

Merry dropped the staff and the light went out. Sucking in a deep breath, she felt around the tunnel floor and scooped up the staff, once again thinking of their need for light. The staff began to glow, making her feel equal parts relieved and anxious. Debra had said her magic could flare out of control if she wasn't trained.

What if she wished for something and the result was worse than a little light?

She pushed that thought down and focused on Ellen instead. 'You couldn't help Debra if you were killed by one of the ghosts.' Even as she said the words Merry knew they would be no comfort. She also felt bad about abandoning the older woman but forced herself to continue in what she hoped was a confident tone.

'She said the ghosts will take care of her once we are gone, and from what I've seen she is a strong woman. I'm sure she'll be okay.' She hoped. And not just because she needed Debra to meet her at the guild tower to help her make the spell to go home. That was even assuming she could get to the other four elemental focal points and get the charms she needed. She slumped against the side of the tunnel, trying not to feel hopeless about what she had to do.

Yes, she now knew she was a witch, and could become a mage with proper training. That didn't mean she was ready to go up against the guild or stop witch hunters from gaining access to the portal her grandmother had guarded. Getting home had never seemed so impossible as it did right then.

But she would find a way back to her reality. She had to.

# CHAPTER 8

With Merry's staff to light the way, they travelled through the tunnel to an exit into a small cave in the hills behind the ruins of Ralinin. Sadie slipped out first to make sure the coast was clear and soon returned to say there was no sign of anyone on this side of the hill. Merry hoped Gabriel and the guild enforcers were still occupied at the boundary of the haunted Spirit enclave, waiting for them to emerge, and that she and her friends would be able to get through the forest without encountering them again.

'The Air focal point is closest,' said Ellen quietly as they navigated the steep and overgrown path from the cave to the floor of the forest. 'We'll head there first.'

*I will scout ahead. Keep your mind open. I will call if there is trouble.* Sadie bounded away, quickly disappearing into the underbrush, as Merry relayed her words to Ellen.

Merry used her staff to steady herself as they

followed in the direction the cat had disappeared. 'How far away is the focal point?'

The map Debra had scratched into the stone floor had given her no idea of scale. For all she knew, Tirana was the size of Australia and it would take them weeks just to get to the first focal point.

'If we make it to Pillingston by nightfall, we can stay there the night and make it to the focal point by lunchtime tomorrow.' Ellen cast a glance at Merry over her shoulder. 'It will be at least two days travel by foot to reach each focal point after that, with Earth the closest to Air. We might be able to shorten the journey if we are able to secure passage with one of the wagon trains merchants use to carry their goods from town to town.'

Two more days to Earth, after they were done with Air, and two more each for Fire and Water. So that would be seven days of travel; unless they found a wagon train to speed their journey. After that they would have to get to the guild tower, and the Spirit focal point beneath it, and only if there were no delays. What must her family be thinking, for her to be missing so long? Did they already have the police looking for her? Her dad had been through this before, as a small child, when her grandmother had disappeared. It had been years before she returned, thanks to her being imprisoned by the guild. Merry was determined that would not happen to her. She would find a way home, one way or the other. Even if that meant she had to learn magic.

Merry flexed her fingers on her staff and when the

path widened enough for her to walk beside Ellen, she tackled the subject.

'Do you know what sort of charm I need to find at the Air focal point and what I'm supposed to do with it to make it magical?' If that was even what she was supposed to do. Debra had been light on details, thanks to the pain she'd been in and trying to stop the vengeful ghosts from harassing Ellen.

'It is different for every witch or mage. When choosing charms for a spell or for other forms of magic, they are often drawn to a particular object.' She waved a hand at Merry's staff. 'Like that. You imbued some of your magic into the branch and formed a magical staff.'

'I didn't mean to. I was just focused on using it to protect myself.' And thinking about Gabriel and his ability to harness the wind, but she didn't want to mention that. He was part of the group trying to capture her. She didn't need to be distracted by thinking about how handsome he was or the guilt at hitting him with the branch to escape.

'Exactly. You were focused on a specific purpose, and your magic helped to create what you needed. Now you will be able to use your staff to focus your intent. As you have an affinity with more than one element, your staff will allow you to do many more things than a staff that was created by someone with only one elemental affinity.'

Things like the light she had used to illuminate the

tunnel, and the wind to push the spirits away, she supposed.

'Part of our training, when our ability first emerges, is to create a focus tool,' said Ellen. 'Some witches make wands, but staffs are popular too.'

Merry frowned. 'You don't have a wand or a staff.'

Ellen flushed, and Merry wondered if she had put her foot in her mouth. Ellen had said she wasn't a strong witch. Maybe she wasn't strong enough to create a focus tool.

Ellen stopped walking and placed a hand on her chest. 'I do have one, but I usually keep it hidden.' She reached into the neckline of her dress and pulled out a silver chain. Dangling on the end of the chain was a teardrop shaped pendant, made from a shimmering stone that reminded Merry of an opal. The colours in this stone swirled against a dark blue background, the movement mesmerising.

'This is heartstone,' said Ellen. 'It can not only help a witch to focus her power, but it can also increase it, depending on the size of the stone.' She shrugged. 'Without it I would be barely more than a field witch. As it is, I still have to speak an incantation to get it to work for me. Mages like you and Debra don't need spoken incantations to get their spells to work.'

Merry, conscious she had stepped on a sore point, simply said, 'It's beautiful.'

'It is also extremely rare and therefore expensive. This one has been in my family for generations or I would never have been given the opportunity to attune myself to one.' She tucked it back in her neckline.

'That's why you put your hand on your chest when you're doing magic,' said Merry.

Ellen nodded. 'Technically, as it is already touching my skin, I don't need to, but I find it helps me focus when I am attempting magic that would be beyond my capabilities normally.'

'So you had to become attuned to the stone, as I did with my staff.' Not that she had thought of it that way when she had been running her hands along the branch and thinking about the pattern she would like to carve into it.

'Yes, though mine was a little more complicated than if I were to have a fresh stone. This one had previously been attuned to my mother. She passed it on to me when it became apparent my ability was with healing. She has an Earth affinity also, but like me she was not strong, and her ability allowed her to interact with butterflies. She could call them to her, covering herself in them, and then get them to fly in certain patterns. It was useful in entertaining small children, but not deemed as useful as being able to heal.'

'That sounds pretty cool though.'

'Perhaps, but there are few people who are willing to barter for something so trivial as dancing butterflies. My augmented herbal remedies help to keep food on the table. There is no point in being able to entertain children when they are too hungry to enjoy it.'

Merry could understand that. Her stomach was empty, and its grumbles were getting louder. 'Speaking of food, does your Earth ability help in finding edible treats in a forest?' Merry smiled as she asked, trying not to let Ellen see just how hungry she was. They had left their food supplies for Debra, who would not be able to find her own easily with a broken ankle.

'Of course it does,' said Ellen with a smile as she placed one hand on her chest and the other on a tree. She closed her eyes, and then a moment later opened them. 'This way,' she said as she set off.

Merry called out to Sadie in her head, and the little cat responded that she was on her way. She caught up with Merry and Ellen when they arrived at a small clearing, with a creek burbling alongside it and bushes filled with round black berries.

*I have seen no sign of humans in this part of the forest. We should be safe to rest for a moment.*

Ellen began harvesting berries as soon as Merry relayed Sadie's message. Merry joined her and they ate as many as they could find, stripping the bush bare of ripe berries, and then Ellen used her magic to imbue cups of creek water with revitalising herbs. Merry felt much better when they set off, even though the meal hadn't been that filling. The magicked water helped to take the edge off her hunger as well as her weariness.

'We'll get a proper meal tonight, at Pillingston,' said Ellen over her shoulder. 'The innkeeper is always willing to give me room and a meal, in return for healing him and his family if they need it and for the extra custom my arrival brings. They have no healer of their own, so I am always busy when I go there.' A frown creased her brow. 'Though I usually have more of my remedies with me when I do.'

She scanned the bushes to either side of the path and started plucking leaves off one of them. 'I'll have to make do with what I have and what I can find along the way.'

Merry knew nothing about herbs, but she helped as best she could, and soon her bag was filled with leaves and flowers Ellen directed her to grab.

It was almost pleasant, now her stomach wasn't complaining so badly, walking through the forest, with Ellen giving a running commentary on the trees and bushes and what medicinal purposes they could be used for, while Sadie scouted ahead. But she couldn't forget that this was not just a jaunt in a forest with a friend. She was on another world, one that had people out to get her.

That fact was driven home when Sadie bounded onto the path in front of them, hackles up on her back. *Enforcers are coming this way.*

Merry grabbed Ellen's arm and the two of them ducked into the bushes where the witch had just been harvesting leaves, moving as quietly as they could.

They had just crouched down and stopped when Merry heard Gabriel's voice. 'It was my decision to abandon the search. My aunt could not want me to risk the lives of her enforcers with an ill-fated incursion of the ruins at Ralinin. She is well aware of the dangers that place poses.'

*If the girl is of the Meadows' bloodline, as we suspect, your aunt would not care how many enforcers died to capture her. She has vowed to bring all those who sided against the guild to justice.*

'Kassandra and the others would have been killed, had I given the order. I will not recklessly risk the lives of those under my command. My aunt wants what is best for the guild. No matter her enmity for those who stood against her, she would not want people to die needlessly.'

*If the girl truly is from the old world, that means a working portal still exists. Your aunt will not give you a warm welcome when you return to the tower and tell her that as well as letting a Meadows witch slip your grasp, you failed to learn the location of the portal she used to get here so it can be destroyed.*

'My aunt will understand. I'm sure of it. Besides, I don't believe Merry poses a threat to the guild. She has no interest in the politics of Tirana. She just wants to return home.'

*She will be a strong mage given training. When your aunt does get her hands on her, and you know she will, you'd better hope your lapse does not bring ruin to us all.*

Gabriel's answer was too low for her to hear, but his familiar's words made Merry worry he would be in trouble when he got to the guild tower. But he hadn't let her go. She'd escaped on her own, hadn't she? Either way, she would need to keep the location of the portal a secret. At least until after she had made a new transportation spell and used it to get back to Belwich. If Sadie was wrong about her being able to renew the wards her grandmother had set, she would find a way to get a message to Gabriel to tell him where the portal was, so he could destroy it and make sure no witch hunters reached Tirana.

She hoped it wouldn't come to that. Destroying the portal would reduce the magic of the bookshop and mean she wouldn't be able to visit the friends she had made. But better that than to put Ellen and Debra at risk.

A shout from down the path came a moment before Kassandra and the other enforcers stepped into view. Kassandra now had some type of bird perched on her arm. A falcon, perhaps. Was that her familiar?

'Gabriel,' said Kassandra. 'Your aunt has sent a message.'

Gabriel strode towards her and stretched out a hand to fiddle with one of the bird's legs. He unrolled a piece of paper and scanned it. 'My aunt wishes us to return to Dryton immediately. Lord Windemere is heading there with his retinue and she wants us to be a show of force, should he be thinking of unwise actions. He and the other lords have been scheming to increase their holdings, with rumours some among them wish to return to having a monarchy. Windemere holds the largest province in the north. If he were to control more of it, he could put himself forward as a candidate for king.'

'The guild will never accept a return to a monarchy,' said Kassandra, scowling.

One of the enforcers groaned. 'Forget about a monarchy. What about stopping in Pillingston for the night, as you said we would?'

Gabriel shook his head. 'There's no time. Lord Windemere will reach Dryton by daybreak.' He wrote something on the note and reattached it to the bird's leg before it took off. Then he headed back the way they had come, and after more groans, the enforcers followed.

Merry and Ellen waited ten minutes before they stepped out from behind their bush. Ellen stood for a long time, looking in the direction Gabriel and the enforcers had taken. It was her town they were now headed to.

'Is this Lord Windemere going to cause trouble?'

Ellen shook her head. 'Not if the enforcers are there. But it's no secret he wishes to expand his territory. The threat of the guild has been keeping him in check, but he has managed to build a considerable army of those who are disenchanted with the way of the world. He even has some magic users on his side, ones that were not powerful enough to garner the attention of the guild but still stronger than the likes of me. If he has enough of them, he might think he could take Dryton if it were not protected.'

With a sigh, she turned away. 'At least we no longer need to worry about the enforcers chasing us. Not this lot anyway. That falcon came from the guild, and Gabriel Fairweather could have asked them to send more enforcers to search for you.'

Merry thought back on Gabriel's conversation with his familiar. From the sounds of it, he had planned to wait until he got to the tower before informing his aunt about her. But maybe that had changed when he had been ordered elsewhere. She had no idea what it was he had added to the note ordering him and the enforcers to Dryton.

With a sigh, she followed Ellen, hoping that was not the case. She had been harried almost from the time she had arrived in Tirana. It would be nice to have one night where she got to relax, and not think about all the obstacles that stood between her and the way home.

Her feet were aching, raw spots rubbed on her heels, when they reached the edge of the forest, while the energising drink had also worn off. Now that they no longer had to walk around trees and bushes, on the rudimentary path they'd been following, the going was much easier. Still, Merry was grateful when she spotted the roofs of low buildings ahead.

Pillingston looked very similar in style to Dryton, though there were more buildings. People were out in the cobbled main street, and a number smiled and waved at them as they made their way to one of the larger buildings. This one had a second storey and the sounds of many people talking came from the other side of an open door. A sign proclaiming it to be Pills Inn hung above the doors.

*I will stay in the stables. Better no one wonders why a companion such as myself would be accompanying a mere witch.* Sadie slipped behind Merry and disappeared down an alley beside the inn, quickly disappearing from sight.

Ellen strode up the three stone steps leading to the doorway and stepped inside, Merry at her back. The interior was brightly lit, lanterns hung on timber beams along the side walls, and a long wooden bar took up most of the wall opposite the doorway. Several tables with timber benches filled the middle of the taproom, many of them occupied by people drinking from wooden mugs. Some had platters of what looked and smelled like roast meat and vegetables in front of them, and Merry's mouth watered.

The portly man behind the bar smiled when he looked over at them. 'Miss Hayland, it is a welcome sight you are.' His eyes moved to Merry, and his smile widened. 'And you have brought another healer.'

Merry stumbled, panic thrumming through her. She wasn't a healer. She wouldn't be expected to heal people, would she?

'I will be pleased to offer my services, to you and others, but Merry has only recently become my apprentice and is still learning. She is here to observe only,' said Ellen.

The innkeeper's face fell, even as Merry was sure relief shone on hers. Then he brightened. 'Come,' he said, 'I am sure you are famished after your journey.' He waved a hand to a table set near one end of the bar.

Two people were already sitting there but he shooed them off. They went with good natured grumbles, as the innkeeper bustled away. He soon returned with a platter of food and two mugs spilling over with a frothy liquid and set them in the middle of the table.

'Eat, drink, please. When you are rested, I will show you to your room.' He looked from Merry to Ellen, a look of chagrin on his face. 'You will require just one room, yes? We are at capacity as it is.'

'Of course,' said Ellen. 'One room is fine.'

The innkeeper smiled and backed away.

Merry surveyed the door to the inn as more people entered. 'If the inn is this busy, how is it he has one room spare for us?'

'He doesn't,' said Ellen. 'We will most likely be sleeping in a storage room. It is what he usually does when the inn is full when I visit. But don't worry, he will give us enough blankets that we won't be uncomfortable.'

Considering the way they had slept the previous night, soaked to the skin and huddled in a hollow made by the roots of a giant tree, anything would be more comfortable. Merry sipped at her drink, and her eyes widened. She had expected it to be some kind of beer, given the froth, but it was actually fruity, more like a cider. Whatever it was, it was tasty and so was the thick slab of bread and cuts of roast meat on the platter. There were roast potatoes and carrots, as well as green beans, and a rich gravy to dunk the food in, though no cutlery. Not that Merry cared about getting her fingers dirty. She was too hungry.

For a long time neither she nor Ellen spoke. Only when the platter was empty, and the last drop of her drink gone, did Merry sit back and focus on the people filling the inn.

More people had entered since last time she'd looked, many of them standing and looking towards their table. They all wore drab clothing and she could see some of them sported bandages, while others looked pale and sickly. The innkeeper was bustling among them, handing out drinks or food to some of them.

Of course, these were the people who had come to see Ellen.

The witch pushed her chair back and stood, beckoning for Merry to follow her through a door at the other end of the bar, one that led into the back of the inn. They walked down a short hallway that was lined with coarse brown sacks of what appeared to be vegetables along the walls. Ellen opened a door and they stepped into a room that smelled strongly of garlic. Shelves along one wall were filled with jars of preserved food. This must be the storeroom, the space that would once have been filled with the sacks of vegetables cleared away and a table with two rickety chairs set behind it in their place.

Ellen placed her bag on the table and then moved back to the door, where her first patient was waiting. What followed was a long line of people with a variety of ailments. Ellen greeted each person with dignity and grace, no matter what their illness was, passing out herbal remedies and slathering salves on wounds, along with instructions on how to continue their care after she left. All through her ministrations she kept up a patter of words explaining to Merry what she was doing and why, to keep up the image that she was her apprentice.

A woman entered with a baby cradled in her arms. The baby was listless, barely making a sound as the woman laid it on the table and Ellen unwrapped the blankets swaddling it and checked it over, hands lingering on the baby's head. For once Ellen did not say anything about what she was doing, while the mother stood on the other side, wringing her hands, face drawn and eyes haunted.

After a moment, Ellen gave a sigh and turned to the mother. 'I'm sorry. There is nothing I can do for her.'

Tears trickled down the mother's cheeks as she gave a nod and wrapped her baby girl up again. Then she turned and left the room without a sound.

Ellen slumped into one of the chairs.

'What was wrong with the baby?' Merry asked.

'Her brain has sustained damage, most likely from a

troubled birth. I could reduce some of the swelling, but to repair the damage that has been done is beyond my abilities. The child will never walk or talk and is not like to last beyond a few years.'

Ellen gave a shake of her head. 'A guild mage would be able to do what I cannot, but would charge more than the mother could raise in ten lifetimes to do so.' She turned to face Merry, tears glistening in her eyes. 'This is why Debra and your grandmother opposed the rule that all mages with strong affinities must be subject to guild law. Only the rich are able to afford the prices the guild charges for magic of a more complex nature. People are dying, babies like that poor little girl, from diseases and afflictions that can be cured, all because they cannot afford to pay. It's not fair. It's wrong. The guild should not be allowed to dictate what a mage chooses to do with magic. But no one is strong enough to oppose them, so innocent people continue to die.'

There was such a look of bleakness in her reddened eyes, that Merry wished there was some way she could help. But not by becoming the powerful mage Ellen and Debra had said she had the potential to become and taking on the guild. Though she hated the thought of the poor baby dying when it could be prevented, and her dislike of the guild strengthened, she was not cut out to be the saviour of a world to which she didn't even belong.

She could not afford to allow herself to be caught up in their struggles. She had to focus on getting home. At least she could do some good there, by renewing the wards around her grandmother's bookshop to stop witch hunters from gaining access to Tirana. Still, nothing would erase her memories of her time in this world, knowing that a little baby and others like her were doomed to die without magical help.

# CHAPTER 9

The mother with the doomed baby was the last patient and Ellen sagged in her rickety chair once she was done.

'You look exhausted,' said Merry.

Ellen gave a weary nod. 'Even with a heartstone, tending to so many people in a row takes it out of me.' She pushed back her chair and stood, swaying slightly. 'Ivan will have a meal ready for us. I'm always starving after an extended healing session.'

At the mention of food, Merry's stomach rumbled. She may not have helped with the healing, but a fair amount of time had passed since they'd eaten earlier. She followed Ellen back to the taproom, where Ivan already had a table set up for them with food and drinks. This time the drink was similar to a hot chocolate though not as sweet, and there were thick slices of a rich fruit cake.

The taproom wasn't as full as it had been earlier, and there were empty platters in front of those who remained. There weren't many women among then, though two sat with a large group of men crowded around a rectangular table on the other side of the large space. The men at the table were boisterous, loud laughs booming out regularly as they conversed. Only the young man sitting at the end of the table furthest away from Merry was quiet. He had shaggy black hair and bushy eyebrows, face unsmiling as he stared back at Merry.

Merry ducked her head, averting her gaze from his unblinking stare.

'Ivan usually pays me a percentage of the takings during my healing sessions, but I'm going to ask him for supplies instead,' said Ellen as she placed her empty mug onto the table and stood. 'I'll see you back at the room.'

Merry stood. 'I'll head back there now,' she said, catching sight of the black-haired man as she moved around the table. His gaze was still on her. No way did she want to stay in the taproom on her own. Ellen headed for the door that led to the kitchen, while Merry entered the hallway and approached the storeroom.

A thin woman with greying hair was rummaging among the jars on the shelf. 'I won't be long, love,' she said with a quick smile to Merry. 'I'll see to your bedding next. If you'd like to leave your clothes by the door I'll see they're cleaned ready for the morning.'

'Thank you,' said Merry, the tension that had built

inside her in the taproom lessening at the thought of clean clothes. She'd been wearing Ellen's spare dress for two days, and it was starting to smell. So was she.

As if the woman had heard Merry's thoughts, she added, 'There's a bathhouse out near the stable. The door at the end of the hall will take you out back. The bathhouse is on the left. I've left clean shifts there for you and Miss Hayland. I understand you had to leave Dryton in a hurry and weren't able to pack.' A lilt of curiosity sounded in her voice, but Merry simply smiled and thanked her again.

She returned to the hall and quickly made her way outside. The night air was cool, and she rubbed her arms as she walked to the bathhouse, quickly working out it was little more than a shed. There was a bucket of cold water on one side and one suspended over a fire in the middle of the shed. An empty bucket sat beside a drain in the stone floor, along with a cake of coarse brown soap and a washcloth.

A rail against one wall held towels and two shapeless calico shifts.

Not exactly what she was used to, but it would do.

After making sure the door was locked behind her, Merry mixed hot and cold water in the empty bucket until she had it at the right temperature, and then stripped off her dirty clothes. It was awkward, but eventually she was as clean as she could get under the circumstances. She would love to be able to wash her hair, but that was not possible in these conditions.

Maybe she would get lucky and their next stop would have better facilities. For now, after she had dressed in the shift, she twisted her hair into a thick plait and tied it in a bun that sat at the nape of her neck.

Then she left the shed, dirty clothes piled in her arms, intending to head back to the room she was to share with Ellen and go to bed.

A shrill cry sounded nearby, so mournful and eerie it had the hairs on her arm standing on end. She gasped and froze. Whatever had made the noise sounded as if it was in pain.

Goose bumps swept over her when the noise came again and she was able to pinpoint the direction. The stable where Sadie had said she was going to hide. The noise didn't sound like a cat. Still, Merry reached out to her grandmother's companion. *Sadie, are you in the stable?*

*No. It was too crowded for my liking. I am curled up near the fire in the inn's kitchen.* A sense of contentment came from the cat. *The innkeeper's wife has a fondness for cats.* A mental yawn sounded in Merry's head.

*You should get some sleep, Merry. You need to take what rest you can. Reaching all the elemental focal points will be an arduous task and this may be the last time you get to sleep without fear of being arrested.*

Merry thought a good night to Sadie as she looked to the back door to the inn, biting her bottom lip. Goose bumps suggested magic was involved with whatever was going on inside the stable. Did she really want to know what was causing it? Whatever was making that sound could not be human, and Sadie was right about her needing to take what rest she could now, while it was safe to do so.

The cry came again, even more mournful and pain-filled than before, making Merry's body quiver with the strength of it. Without conscious thought, her feet took her to the door of the stable and she peered inside. A lantern hung on a hook beside the door, allowing her to see several stalls. The shifting of hooves and troubled neighs indicated they were occupied, and possibly just as perturbed by the sound as she was. It came again, from a stall at the very end, and the horses tossed their heads, nostrils flaring, manes flying. One even kicked at its stall door, making it shake alarmingly.

That horse was the one stabled closest to whatever was making the mournful noise.

Merry crept closer and peered inside the last stall. The door was open, allowing her to see a wire cage half her height resting on the straw strewn ground, with a dark shape huddled within. The pungent aroma of horse manure tickled her nose and she sneezed. Whatever was trapped in the cage gave a low squawk and shuffled around.

It was a huge bird, with silver and grey speckled wings, but the confines of the cage made it impossible for it to spread them. Its head bumped the top of the cage as it stared at Merry, setting sparks flying, and it gave the mournful cry. Goose bumps swept over Merry again and she gasped. The cage was electrified, or whatever the magical version was. Every time the bird touched the walls or ceiling, it received what had to be a painful shock.

Who would do such a thing?

Merry crouched down as she stared at the bird. It had such a regal air to it, but its eyes were filled with sorrow as it surveyed her. Then its gaze dropped, the beak aiming towards a latch on the side of the cage door. Then it looked back to Merry.

'You want me to let you out?'

The bird bobbed its head.

It was intelligent. Maybe not as intelligent as Sadie or the other familiars she had encountered, but still. No one should cage a bird that could make its wishes so clearly known. Especially not in a cage too small and that would shock it every time it touched the walls or ceiling.

Merry took a deep breath and reached for the lock, wondering if the magic would shock her. But all she felt was a slight tingle in her fingers as she unlocked it and swung the door open. She scrambled backward as the bird slowly manoeuvred its way out of the opening, careful not to touch the sides. Once it was free, it unfurled its wings, the draught the movement created swirling the soft tendrils of hair around her face. The bird tucked its wings in again and shuffled in close, delicately placing its beak over her arm. Then it backed off and worked its way out of the stall. Once it was free, it spread its wings again and flew out the stable doors, vanishing from sight.

Merry closed the cage door, scrambled to her feet, and headed out of the stable, hoping she wouldn't get in trouble for freeing the bird. A shadow swept over her as she made her way to the inn door and she looked up to see the bird hovering in the air above her.

No.

It was not the bird she had freed.

This one was full silver, the feathers shining brightly in the light of the moon. It came down so close Merry thought it was going to land on her head, but it angled away at the last second. She caught sight of the bird she had freed as the silver one joined it and then the two of them flew off into the night. With a sigh, Merry headed inside, pleased to find two piles of bedding on the storage room floor. Ellen was there, and quickly headed off for her own bath, giving Merry no time to tell her what had just happened. Perhaps it was better that way. If no one knew how the bird had escaped, Merry might avoid more trouble.

By the time Ellen returned, and they both placed their dirty clothes outside the room to be cleaned, Merry was so tired she could barely keep her eyes open. She gratefully lay down in one pile of blankets and closed her eyes.

She was sure she had only just gone to sleep when Ellen woke her and handed her the clean dress. 'Ivan has arranged for us to join a merchant group travelling to sell their wares at this season's markets on the coast. We will need to part ways with them at the crossroad leading to Breezeway, the town built close to the Air focal point, but at least it will give us some cover in case the guild sent more people to search for us. We leave immediately after breakfast.'

Merry rubbed the sleep from her eyes as she got up, then quickly dressed. It felt good to be wearing clean clothes again, and she wished she'd thought to put her shorts and t-shirt out to be cleaned as well, but then the strange garments would probably attract too much attention from the innkeeper's wife.

She followed Ellen to the taproom and was enjoying a mug of tea and fresh baked ham and eggs when the black-haired man who had been staring at her the night before walked up to their table.

This time he looked to Ellen as he said, 'Master Gin is almost ready to go.'

'Of course,' said Ellen, pushing back her chair and standing. 'We'll just grab our things and meet you out front.' She gestured for Merry to follow her.

As she went Merry was conscious that he was now watching her and she stifled a grimace, not pleased to know they would be travelling with him. Though, at least they would not have to go all the way to the Air focal point with him and the merchant he worked for. Even a short time with him, if he kept staring at her, was bound to make her uncomfortable.

She and Ellen retrieved their things from the storage

room and then headed to the kitchen. It was warm in there, embers blazing in the fireplace set in the back wall with what looked like a pig on a spit set up over it. Sadie was stretched out on her side in front of the fire. While Ellen accepted two bags of provisions from Ivan and his wife, Merry sidled over to the cat, holding her hands out as if to warm them, not wanting to ruin Sadie's act as a pet cat.

*We're ready to leave. We're travelling with a group of merchants. Ellen said we will travel as far as the crossroad that leads to Breezeway with them.*

Sadie gave a stretch, rolled over and then sat on her haunches and delicately licked one paw before proceeding to wash her face. *I will find a place to hide among their wagons and join you once we have parted company with the merchants.* The black cat got up and sauntered to the door that led to the hall, brushing against Merry's leg as she went, her sleek black fur warmed by the fire.

Ellen and Merry said goodbye to their hosts and then ventured out the front of the inn. In the street, Merry saw the horses from the stables hitched to three wagons, one of which had the empty cage in among a jumble of casks and crates.

A grey-haired man stood beside that wagon, gesturing at the empty cage while yelling at a rangy teenager. 'I told you to make sure the damned thing was watched. It would have fetched a good price when we got to the coast markets. Now all I have to show for the effort it took to trap the damned thing is an empty cage. How much do you think that will fetch me at market? Huh?'

The boy mumbled something in return, hanging his head, and Merry felt bad for being responsible for his trouble. But she did not regret freeing the bird. A creature like that did not belong in a cage or being sold off to the highest bidder. She hurried after Ellen as she headed to the last wagon, wondering if this was the one where Sadie was hiding.

*Sadie, where are you?* Merry asked as she lifted the hem of her dress and clambered into the back of the wagon.

*Here.* The cat peeked out from behind a small barrel and Merry smiled, pleased she had made it. Then she stifled a groan when she looked to the front of the wagon and realised the black-haired stranger was the one driving it.

She and Ellen settled in the back, nestled among Master Gin's goods, and soon the wagon train set off. The two women she had seen the night before were in the back of the first wagon, as was the boy who had got in trouble for losing the bird. Master Gin sat beside the driver of the lead wagon, turning every now and then to glare at the boy.

The wagons trundled through town and Merry shaded her eyes as she looked about her. This was the first time since she had arrived in Tirana that she hadn't been in a hurry and could look about her. Not that there was much to see. The people who were out and about seemed to be as drab as their clothing, and she remembered the haggard faces of those who had come to Ellen for healing the day before. Only Ivan and his wife had shown any good cheer, and the merchants they were now travelling with.

The stone cottages lining either side of the road heading out of town were just as rundown as the people who lived in them, the land around each one turned into a vegetable garden. These people were poor and in ill health, and according to Ellen it was because of the stranglehold the guild kept on the mages with stronger abilities. Only witches like her were left to tend to those unable to afford to pay guild prices; people such as the mother of the baby that Ellen had said would not live to see her second birthday.

'So, you're a healer.'

The brusque words jolted Merry from her thoughts. She looked up, expecting the comment to have been directed at Ellen, but the wagon driver was peering over his shoulder at her.

'Er, I'm an apprentice.'

He smirked. 'Aren't you a little old to be an apprentice?'

She narrowed her eyes. 'No.'

'Where are you headed? Old Gin said you're leaving us at the crossroad.'

Merry looked to Ellen, who said agreeably, 'We'll be

visiting colleagues in Cambleyn, to continue Merry's training.'

Cambleyn was not the town they were headed to, but Merry hoped the information would shut him up.

He faced the road for a while, and then twisted back. 'I'm Travis. You're Merry, right? With a name like that, shouldn't you smile more?'

'As a wagon driver, shouldn't you face the front?'

'Scenery's prettier this way,' he said with a wink.

'Yes, it is,' said Merry, turning around and facing the back of the wagon, ignoring his low chuckle at her response.

It was a pretty scene, now that they had left town. Green fields with yellow flowers flowed on either side of the road, while in the distance stood a stand of tall trees. The air was fresh and crisp, birds singing and butterflies flitting above the flowers. If not for the stress and urgency of her mission, she might actually enjoy the ride. That is, if the buffoon driving the wagon left her alone.

Travis made a few more attempts to flirt with her, but she ignored him, leaving it to Ellen to field his questions. Eventually he lapsed into silence and Merry allowed herself to relax back against the side of the wagon. Ellen unrolled her satchel of herbs and began describing their medicinal uses and how to prepare various brews or ointments with them. Some of it Merry remembered from the running commentary Ellen had given as she had foraged on their way to

Pillingston and then tended to the villagers, but most of it was new.

Though she was sure Ellen had started the explanations as a way to deter more questions from the driver and to counter his doubt about her being an apprentice healer, Merry found herself enjoying the impromptu lesson. She held various dried herbs to her nose, working to differentiate between them by their smell and texture. Ellen had her repeat back what she remembered about each one.

'When we get to Cambleyn I'll take you foraging again,' said Ellen, 'as there are different varieties to be found there than back home.'

'And where is home, exactly?'

Merry had almost forgotten about the driver, and her jaw tightened as she glared up at him.

Smirking, Travis said, 'In case I ever need a healer while I'm in these parts. Your teacher there sounds like someone who knows her stuff.'

'We're from Dryton,' said Ellen.

His eyebrows rose. 'Really? See, I've been through there before and I do remember seeing you. But I can't say I've ever seen your apprentice before, and I'm sure I would remember seeing Merry.' He drew out the syllables in her name and Merry narrowed her eyes.

'Maybe I didn't want to be seen,' she said.

'And why would that be, hm? Pretty girl like you, wouldn't take to being shut away, I reckon.'

'Merry's father was overprotective,' said Ellen. 'This is also why she has not been my apprentice for long.'

Travis sent Ellen a considering look and then opened his mouth to say something else but the wagon wheel hit a bump in the dirt road and he turned to the front to control it.

'There's the crossroad,' said Ellen, pointing ahead.

Merry was pleased to know they would soon be parting ways with the nosy driver.

As the wagons pulled up in a clearing beside the road, she realised all the wagons were stopping. Master Gin was out, directing the young boy he'd berated for losing the caged bird to fill water casks from a nearby stream, while the two women were spreading out packages of food on a blanket on the grass. Their wagon pulled up in the clearing and Sadie lithely slipped out from behind the barrel and darted into nearby bushes.

Merry's muscles twinged as she clambered down, ignoring the driver's offer to assist her as she looked to see if anyone had noticed the black cat. She gave a sigh of relief to see they were all occupied with stretching to work out the kinks from sitting in one position for so long.

Ellen climbed down from the wagon with much more grace than Merry had employed and started walking towards the two women. When Travis jumped down and moved towards Merry, she quickly set off after Ellen. When she got closer to the other women, she realised they had to be mother and daughter, and when the boy returned with the full cask, he called the older woman, "Mother".

As Master Gin joined his family, Ellen waved a hand at the cask. 'If you permit, I will treat the water.'

Approval was readily given, and the cask was soon filled with energising water. Merry gulped down the mugful Ellen handed to her, not realising how thirsty she had become while sitting in the back of the wagon. She was also hungry, and gladly accepted the offer to share in the family's meal. She was even more pleased when Travis moved off to stand with the others in the wagon train.

Once the meal was done, the family packed up and began stowing the items they had used back into the first wagon. Merry gave an audible groan when Travis came over to stand beside her.

'I guess you and your teacher will be off now, to Cambleyn,' he said, indicating his head to the sign in the middle of the crossroad. Arrows marked the roads that led to Breezeway, Cambleyn and Pillingston, as well as a place called Blackstone Harbour, presumably where the coastal markets were to be held.

Ellen stepped up with an easy smile on her face. 'Actually, we are going to do some foraging first.' She waved a hand at the bushes around the clearing where they had lunched. 'There are some lovely specimens here Merry can use to start her own herb collection.'

He opened his mouth to say something else but Master Gin called out for him to stop dawdling. With a disgruntled expression he headed back to his wagon and launched himself into the driver's seat. Soon after that the wagon train set off, and Merry and Ellen were left standing in the clearing on their own. She was conscious of Travis staring back at her until the curve of the road took him from her sight.

When there was no one left to see, Sadie slipped out of the bushes to join them. Then the three of them started walking down the road that led to Breezeway and the Air focal point. Merry just hoped she would be able to recognise the charm she needed. The sooner she found it and they started the journey to the next focal point the better.

The buzz from Ellen's enchanted water kept Merry going as they tramped down the dirt road that led to Breezeway. It was a beautiful day, and she found herself relaxing as they walked. Every now and then Ellen would stop to pick a flower or leaf and explain the properties to Merry before she tucked it away in her satchel, while Sadie amused herself by chasing butterflies and other small insects, tail twitching as she stalked her prey.

Merry smiled at the cat's antics. It seemed being a companion didn't prevent her from being as playful as a less refined cat.

She turned to Ellen. 'I appreciate you taking my cover story as your apprentice seriously, but there is no one here but us. You don't need to keep pretending to teach me.'

Ellen flushed. 'Sorry, I thought you might like to know this stuff. I'll stop.'

Merry's stomach fell at the hurt tone in her friend's voice. 'No, I do want to know it. It could come in handy, while I'm stuck here. I just didn't want you to think you had to teach me.'

'Oh no. I love teaching.' Ellen's expression brightened. 'There's been no one else in my village who had any aptitude for healing or the interest, so it's wonderful to be able to talk to someone about it. And if Debra is right about you being like your grandmother and having an aptitude for all five elements, then you could really become a healer.'

Merry wasn't so sure about that. She may have been able to create a staff and use it to ward off ghosts, but what she had seen Ellen do back at the inn seemed far more complicated, even if the healer kept insisting she wasn't a strong witch. But she was going out of her way to help Merry, so if this was what Ellen wanted then she was happy to be her apprentice for the short time she was in Tirana.

She *hoped* it would be a short time!

'How much longer until we reach Breezeway?'

Ellen looked at the sky and then scanned the terrain around them. 'We should get there well before sundown, if we don't run into any delays.'

'Great,' said Merry.

They had had the road to themselves, though she caught sight of someone tending to a flock of sheep in a hilly field a short distance away. The land around them was filled with rolling hills covered in lush green grass. It reminded her of a ski trip she had taken to the South Island of New Zealand with a group of school friends after they finished high school. She could even see snow-capped mountains in the distance back the way they had come, the vibrant green landscape far different from the often dry and brown colours she was used to from living in an area that was often in drought. It was much cooler here than it was back home, too, which helped to make the journey on foot more comfortable.

A wind was picking up around then, cooling her even further as they walked, but she soon forgot about that as Ellen coached her in an attempt to sense the power inherent in the earth around them.

'The first thing an Earth witch is taught is to connect with their element. You have already made a connection with Air, while using your staff at Ralinin. Now I want you to concentrate on the ground beneath your feet, feel yourself sinking into it with each step. Immerse yourself in the soil that nourishes us all.'

Ellen's words swept over Merry, and she found herself running her hands over the staff as she walked. It warmed beneath her fingers as the wind picked up strength. Was she doing that, creating the wind?

She was supposed to be connecting with the Earth element.

Merry pushed aside thoughts of the wind and let her hands relax on the staff, concentrating on the scents resounding in the air. It was fresh, crisp, no exhaust fumes or other smells she associated with living in a technologically advanced world. Wherever Tirana was, it didn't mirror the world she had come from.

It had a richness to it, a sense of longevity and serenity that soaked into her. As Ellen had suggested, she concentrated on the ground she walked on, feeling the way the dirt shifted under her boots, tiny pebbles skittering away. Lush green grasses in the fields on either side of the road swayed, the soil they were embedded in far richer and moister than the dirt in the well-travelled road. She could feel the roots embedded in the soil, drinking in nourishment even as the sun helped to fuel them.

A deep sigh escaped Merry's lips at the sensation of completeness she felt from the grass, a longing to lie down among it and join in the cycle of nature. A hard gust of wind pushed at her, and the feeling of oneness with the earth vanished.

She stumbled, and Ellen reached out to steady her, a wide smile on her face. 'You did it.'

Had she? Or had it merely been her imagination? She didn't know enough about how magic worked to tell.

Ellen must have seen the doubt on her face as she said, 'I could feel you, as part of my connection to the earth. Debra was right, you do have more than one elemental affinity. I'll make a healer of you yet.'

She sounded so happy that Merry didn't remind her that she wasn't staying. As soon as she had the charms she needed, and Debra helped her to make a new transportation spell, she was leaving Tirana and might never be able to return. Not if she couldn't renew the wards protecting the portal and it had to be destroyed. She gripped her staff tightly, aware how many obstacles stood in the way of her getting home. But she would make it.

As if to remind her of her own insignificance, the wind gusted around her again, stronger than before. The trees lining the road shook, branches creaking as they were blown about, leaves and small twigs flung into the air and then falling to the ground. The staff was cool so Merry knew this was not her doing. It had to be a natural wind.

Then again…

'Is it always like this, close to the Air focal point?' Merry asked.

Ellen shook her head as she scanned the sky, brow furrowed. 'All the elements are dormant, unless a witch or mage works with them, and I don't think this wind is natural.'

Merry blanched. The only other person she had met that could control the wind was Gabriel Fairweather. 'Do you think it's the guild, trying to stop us from reaching the focal point for the Air leyline?'

The wind had grown increasingly stronger, and Merry had to lean forward to make any headway. Even with Ellen's magic water sloshing around in her stomach, she found her energy levels flagging.

'He and the others wouldn't have beaten us here, or we would have seen them. But someone is playing with the wind,' said Ellen, worry coating her voice, along with the effort it was taking to continue walking.

*At this rate, it will take us twice as long to get to Breezeway.*

Sadie's mental voice sounded strained, and Merry looked to see the black cat was walking low to the ground, her sleek fur ruffled by the wind.

'Can you do something?' Ellen shouted, her words whipped away by the wind, making them hard to hear even though they were side by side.

'Me?' Merry gulped at the thought of trying to control wind of this magnitude. She had swept aside a couple of ghosts, sure, but this was another thing entirely.

She looked over to Sadie again. The cat had stopped moving, and was hunched down on her belly, ears flattened. As she watched, a gust of wind pushed her back even as it lifted her front paws off the ground. Merry bent down and reached out a hand to catch the cat before she went flying off. With a yowl, Sadie dug her claws into Merry's shoulder.

Merry wrapped her free arm around the cat, trying to shield her from the wind, as she held the staff braced in front of her. Ellen gave a scream as she was pushed back and she stretched out a hand and grabbed hold of Merry's other shoulder, huddling in close. She had no idea what it was Ellen expected her to be able to do, but she had to do something. They were all going to be blown away if she didn't. Even now the wind pushed and pulled at the arm securing Sadie to her chest.

Closing her eyes, Merry held up the staff and tried to imagine a bubble of air encasing her and her friends; a cocoon of air that the wind could not penetrate. Nothing happened, the wind seeming to push and pull at them with even more ferocity.

Merry gritted her teeth and gave a guttural roar, clenching her fingers around the staff and mentally commanding the wind to stop.

Sudden silence fell.

Opening her eyes, Merry gaped at what she saw.

The wind still blew, the trees bending over with the force of the gusts, the grass almost flattened to the ground. But the space around Merry and the others was calm, no wind stirring near them at all, and no sound reaching them.

'You did it.' Awe filled Ellen's voice as she let go of Merry and took a small step to the side, surveying the two-metre-wide space around them that was blissfully free of the roaring wind.

Merry grimaced, the warmth of the staff between her fingers pulsing in time with her heartbeat. 'I don't know how long I can hold it.' Her arm was already starting to shake.

'Run,' said Ellen, once again reaching out to hold Merry's shoulder.

It was awkward, huddled together, and Merry had to

concentrate on maintaining her bubble with each step, but they went as fast as they could. The pain in her shoulder where Sadie's claws were still dug in grew, but Merry didn't let go. If she dropped the shield, bubble, whatever it was she had created around them, the little cat would be swept away by the ferocious wind that battered against the world around them.

Her legs felt like jelly, barely able to hold her weight, and Ellen had gone from holding on to her shoulder to helping to hold Merry up as their pace slowed. Stumbling, dizziness washing over her in waves, Merry looked ahead for some kind of shelter, somewhere they could ride out the storm. Surely whoever had created the wind had to be tiring. She was about to collapse after holding her bubble for only a short time, so they had to be about to collapse as well. Unless they were far stronger and better trained than Merry.

This, given she had no idea what she was doing, was highly possible.

Maybe with training, she would be able to effortlessly hold her bubble for hours on end. But for now, she knew she was at breaking point. She would not be able to hold it much longer, leaving the three of them to the mercy of the wind once more.

'We're almost there,' said Ellen. 'You just need to hold on a little longer.'

Sweat stung Merry's eyes as she looked to see how far they had to go. Up ahead was a small river, with a curved stone bridge spanning its width. A stone building that reminded Merry of a tiny castle, complete with a tower, stood on the other side of the bridge.

If they could make it over the bridge, and get inside the building, they would be safe.

She groaned as she forced her legs to move faster, flashes of light in her eyes warning her she was at her limit. They were halfway across the bridge when the bubble collapsed. Sadie yowled as the wind tried to pull her out of Merry's arms, and her claws dug in even further. Merry screamed at the flash of pain, using the adrenaline it brought to launch herself to the end of the bridge. She could no longer feel Ellen at her side, and when she reached the side of the building and gained a small respite from the wind she spun around.

Ellen was still on the bridge, on all fours, as she attempted to crawl across. A bang behind Merry showed a wooden door that was half broken off its hinges. She shoved Sadie through the doorway along with her staff, and then bent over double as she ran back to Ellen, clutching the side of the bridge in one hand. She grabbed Ellen by the shoulder and pulled her back with her until they were both in the shadow of the building.

Then, heart pounding, breath coming in gasps, she urged Ellen through the doorway and followed her inside. The second the force of the wind was shut out, her legs collapsed under her and she hit the stone floor hard.

'Merry!'

Ellen was at her side in an instance, hastily

rummaging in her satchel. 'I don't have time to mix a potion. You'll need to chew the leaves. But don't swallow them.'

Dizziness stole her vision as Merry felt her mouth being pried open and something shoved inside.

'You need to chew, Merry. It's the only thing to help with magic exhaustion.'

At Ellen's urging, Merry closed her eyes and began to chew, gagging at the bitter taste of the leaves. As the gag inducing juice from the leaves slipped down the back of her throat, the feeling she was about to pass out faded and she was able to open her eyes. Not that she felt like getting up anytime soon.

'You can spit the leaves out now,' said Ellen, relief in her tone.

Merry leaned to the side and spat out the wad of chewed up leaves onto the stone floor. She'd clean up the mess she'd made later. Much later. She propped herself up against the wall and looked to where Sadie and Ellen wore matching expressions of concern on their faces.

Sadie's whiskers twitched, ears alert. *Overextending yourself like that was dangerous. You could have been killed, if the healer didn't have runeleaf.*

'That would have been good to know *before* I got into a battle with gale force winds.'

'Uh?'

At the perplexed look in Ellen's face, Merry explained what Sadie had said.

'She's right. I should have warned you, but I never expected you to be able to channel so much power, not without training.' Guilt coloured her words and brimmed in her eyes. 'I'm so sorry.'

'It's okay,' said Merry. 'We all would have been smashed to pieces by that wind if I hadn't done something.' Not that she fully understood what it was she had done.

As strength slowly returned to her limbs, she looked at Ellen. 'When I stopped the wind, I imagined a bubble forming around us, protecting us. Is that how magic works for you?'

Ellen nodded. 'It works on your intent, depending on the strength of your affinity with the element you are aligned to. When I mix my potions or ointments, I think about increasing the strength of the ingredients, to make them more powerful. A guild healer can concentrate on the injury or illness and focus their energy on direct healing. But when I try that, all I can manage is simple healing, like easing a headache or healing a small wound.'

'How do you go with claw marks?' Merry winced as she moved the shoulder Sadie had been attached to.

To her relief, Ellen did fine with claw marks and she was soon feeling no pain, in her shoulder at least. The rest of her body ached, and she felt weak enough a slight breeze would knock her over, let alone the gale still underway outside.

'The Air focal point is on the other side of the

village,' said Ellen. 'But there's no way we will make it with this wind. We'll have to hope it stops soon, so we can get there.'

That suited Merry fine. She watched as Ellen parcelled out some of the food Ivan had given them. As she munched on the thick roast beef sandwiches and sipped a mug of Ellen's magicked water, some of her weariness fell away. She still wished for a soft bed to lie on, so she could sleep for a week.

Beside her, Sadie delicately nibbled at slices of beef, and then Merry placed her mug on the stone floor so the cat could lap up the last of the water. Ellen was packing the mugs away when the wind outside ceased, the silence almost deafening without it.

Merry's eyes widened as she stared at Ellen. Was the wind really gone, or would it start up again the moment they set foot outside their refuge?

Only one way to find out.

Merry dragged herself to her feet, grateful when Ellen picked up the staff and handed it to her. Leaning heavily on the staff, she made her way to the door. The staff felt warm, and holding it made her feel more alert as she stepped outside, as though it was giving energy back to her. Each step made her feel that bit stronger, but still not able to wrestle with the wind if it returned.

The village buildings were all made from the same grey stone as those in every other place she had been, with the same conical roofs, but the village had taken extensive damage in the wind. Window shutters were broken as well as doors, and stones had fallen from roofs and walls, while there was evidence of the wind's ferocity all around them in overturned buckets, uprooted plants and a general air of disarray.

The cobbled street was empty and there was no sign of the villagers as they made their way through. Now that the wind had subsided, Merry would have thought the people would have come out to assess the damage, but no one had appeared by the time they reached the last of the buildings.

Suddenly she heard angry shouting coming from ahead of them. She shared an anxious glance with Ellen as they made their way down a worn path that led between two low hills. They emerged in a large clearing on the other side of the hills, to find it filled with over a hundred people wearing drab-coloured clothes. There was no white, so none of them could have been the one who had caused the windstorm.

Beyond the crowd of people there was a swirling shape in the air and it almost looked like the shape of a person. A giant person made of fog.

'Oh no,' said Ellen, a hand going to her mouth. 'Someone has summoned a wind golem. No wonder the wind was so strong.'

*A wind golem?*

Merry peered closer at the swirling shape, detecting holes that stood for eyes and a gaping mouth. 'What's a wind golem?'

'An elemental sprite that is very strong and

extremely difficult to control. To have one here, right above the Air focal point, is really bad.' She reached out and clutched Merry's arm. 'The only way to subdue one is with a sacrifice. We need to leave, now.'

Even as she said the words, someone in the crowd of villagers turned and spotted them. He gave a shout and soon all the people standing in the clearing were looking at Merry and her friend. Ellen tugged on her arm and she turned to run, but her legs were still too wobbly to go much faster than a walk. All too soon they were overtaken by a pack of villagers. They were quickly surrounded, and as Merry surveyed the mix of fear and anger on their faces her stomach sank.

Ellen had said a sacrifice was needed to appease the wind golem. She hoped that didn't mean what she thought it did. A tall, wide man pushed through the crush of people surrounding them and waved his hands for silence.

'I am Mayor Crighton. Is this your doing?' His brows were lowered, anger in his gaze as he pointed at the golem.

'Of course not,' said Ellen, her voice shaking. 'We're healers. Not Air witches.' She waved a hand at her green dress, and then pointed to the one Merry wore.

Suspicion narrowed his gaze. 'Someone summoned the golem, and you two are the only strangers we've seen for three days.'

'I swear, we only just arrived. We knew nothing about the golem, or we wouldn't have come,' said Ellen.

At her words, the suspicion left the man's gaze and the tension in his broad frame relaxed.

Then a woman with tears streaming down her face pushed through to stand beside him, stretching out a hand to point to Merry and Ellen. 'We can sacrifice one of them, Mayor Crighton. Not my Lindy. She doesn't deserve to be swallowed by a wind golem.'

Uh oh.

# CHAPTER 11

The crowd jostled Merry and she stumbled sideways, colliding with Ellen. They shared a scared glance, before Ellen held up her hands and faced the woman who wanted to sacrifice them to the wind golem.

'There's no need to sacrifice anybody. The mage who summoned the wind golem can send it back. You just have to find them.'

'Do you think we haven't tried that?' the woman cried out, wringing her hands. 'The wind golem has been terrorising our town for three days, demanding a sacrifice. We've hunted everywhere for whoever summoned it. But it's no use. Whoever they are, they either left immediately after summoning it, or they're hidden too well for us to ever find them. If we don't stop the golem now, it will destroy our village.'

Many in the crowd murmured their agreement, and

Merry swallowed hard at the dark mood flowing from them. Mayor Crighton nudged the distraught mother aside and shook his head. 'Margaret is right. We don't have time to find whoever is responsible or wait for someone from the guild to arrive to disperse the golem.'

His expression soured. 'If they would even lift a finger to help us. There are those who suspect they are the ones who summoned it. The enforcer who came to collect our recent tithe said the guild were unhappy with what we offered them last time and demanded more. More we could not give. He said the guild would withhold their protection if the new tithe was not met. Then he left. A day later the golem appeared.'

Angry mutters rose around them at his words, and Merry heard many of them cursing the guild. It seemed the mayor was right in saying many of them believed the guild were responsible for the golem's arrival.

The woman who had suggested either Merry or Ellen be sacrificed instead of her daughter, gave a bitter laugh. 'The guild will never help us. They want us punished for defying them. What better punishment than to make us sacrifice one of our own?'

'Please,' said Ellen, hands still held out in entreaty in front of her. 'I'm sure the guild does not want you to sacrifice anyone. If you sent for their help three days ago, they can't be too far away.'

The mayor shook his head again. 'The enforcer made it clear we had lost guild protection when we could not double our tithe. If the guild didn't make the golem, they would not help us, even if we had sent a messenger to beg for aid. We have to do something now.' Sorrow darkened his expression as he looked at Ellen. 'I'm sorry. But a sacrifice must be made, and you are strangers.'

'Perhaps we can help. Merry has—'

He held up his hand. 'As you said, you are healers. Not Air witches. Besides, if either of you were strong enough to take on a wind golem you'd be part of the guild.' He waved at their clothes. 'But you are not mages.'

'You don't understand. Merry can control the wind. Look at her staff.' Ellen waved for Merry to hold it up.

Mayor Crighton leaned in, brows lowered as he stared at the staff. His eyes widened when Merry made it glow, but then he shook his head. 'If she can create such a powerful focus tool, why is she wearing a witch's dress? She should be wearing a guild robe.'

'Her clothes were destroyed in a fire. She is wearing my dress until we can get her new clothes, and she has only recently come into her powers. She has not been sworn to the guild yet. Please, let her try to appease the wind golem before you talk of sacrificing anyone.'

At her words, the hard lump in Merry's throat lurched. She barely knew what she was doing. How was she supposed to take on a wind golem? She cast a look over her shoulder and could see the top half of the golem over the heads of those surrounding them. It swirled in the air, one second appearing as a roiling bundle of clouds and the next forming human features. But in whatever form it took, it projected an air of malevolence. There was no way she would be able to disperse it.

The mayor was clearly of the same mind. His eyes narrowed as he asked, 'How can a girl who has just come into her powers have any chance against that?' He flung out a hand and pointed at the golem.

Ellen gave Merry a pleading look and then said, 'Merry is the granddaughter of Meredith Meadows.'

Gasps met her words and Merry found herself the recipient of many stares. Uncomfortable stares, tinged with a mixture of awe, hope and disbelief. While she knew why Ellen had announced her bloodline, the expectation that came with being related to her grandmother felt smothering.

After a long moment while his gaze bored into Merry, Mayor Crighton stepped back and waved a hand. 'Let her through,' he said. 'We'll see how she goes against the golem.' From his tone, he didn't hold out much hope that a mage newly coming into her abilities would be able to do anything against the threat the wind golem posed, no matter what her bloodline.

As the crowd at her back shuffled sideways, clearing the way between her and the chasm, Merry didn't blame him for being sceptical. She turned to face the wind golem, with no idea what she was supposed to do now. The villagers surged forward, and she was pushed along at their head, closer and closer to the wind golem. She looked over her shoulder for Ellen, but the mayor had a firm grip on her friend's arm, holding her back. If Merry couldn't defeat the golem, she was sure he would push ahead with the sacrifice.

*A wind golem is powerful magic, but you have your grandmother's spirit.*

Merry couldn't see Sadie but was grateful for the soothing touch of her mental voice.

*What am I supposed to do?* she thought back to the little cat.

*Use the power you have bound to your staff and draw on the golem's substance. If you can channel the wind at its centre, you will be able to control it.*

If.

Merry did not like her chances. She still felt weak from fighting the wind to get to Breezeway, but she had to give it a try. She held up the staff in front of her, hands spaced a shoulder width apart, as she sought to feel the wind that comprised the golem, seeing the centre. As when Ellen had directed her to connect with the earth beneath her feet on the way here, she cast out her senses.

Nothing happened, so she closed her eyes and tightened her focus to the wind that swelled in the depths of the chasm, spilling over to buffet those standing in the clearing. In her mind, her eyes traced the swirls and dips of the wind, seeking the source. As she concentrated, the staff warmed beneath her palms. She opened her eyes and was drawn to a swirling vortex in the middle of the golem's head, between the gaping holes that were its eyes.

Was this what Sadie meant? She had expected the centre to be in the torso. She sent a mental query to the cat.

*For a golem, as with any creature, the centre is what the mage who summoned it uses to control it.*

Merry's jaw tightened. She would have to channel its brain, to have any hope of wresting control from someone who was both more powerful and knowledgeable than she was. She took a deep breath and then held it as she focused on the vortex in the golem's head.

*Obey me.*

Her command resonated inside her head for a brief moment, and then a whooshing sound swept over her. She reeled, sure the wind was returning, but the roar was muted, distant. Her vision blurred and she became disoriented, making her think she was seeing two different things. As her vision slowly cleared, she could still see two images, one superimposed on other. She was looking at the golem. At the same time, she could see the people crowded at her back on the edge of the chasm.

She was seeing through the golem's eyes.

How gaping holes in a creature composed of air could see was beyond her. Not that it mattered. What was important was that she had somehow managed to get inside the golem's centre. Maybe they weren't that hard to control after all. She sharpened her focus, working on doing what Sadie had suggested, and mentally commanding the golem to disperse.

It was a weird sensation, to be aware of her own body, and yet seeing out of two sets of eyes, but she smiled when she felt a lessening of the wind that had been swirling in the chasm depths.

It was working. The golem was starting to shrink.

Then a fresh gust of wind came from the heart of the chasm, roaring up and over the edge, racing towards Merry. She swung her staff and the wind split around her, knocking the people at her back over even as it changed directions. Merry was safe, the staff creating a cocoon around her, but the others weren't so lucky.

The wind buffeted them about, and their arms flailed as they sought to balance themselves, some of them coming uncomfortably close to the edge of the chasm. Merry had no time to worry about them. She no longer had two images in her head. She had lost the connection with the golem, and it was swirling even more violently than before, gaping mouth open in a roar that carried with it a blast of frozen air. Merry held up the staff, willing it to shield her. It flared painfully hot in her palms, though the outsides of her hands were chilled.

The blast stopped and Merry sank to her knees, using the staff to keep herself from toppling on her face as the golem thrashed in the air in front of her.

'It's no use,' someone shouted. 'She isn't strong enough.'

Merry was too weary to turn around to see who had spoken, arms and legs shaking as if she had just run a marathon.

'We have to go through with the sacrifice,' said Mayor Crighton.

A surge of adrenaline swept through Merry at his words, giving her the energy to lurch to her feet and swing about to face the crowd, staff raised as she prepared to fight them off. They weren't looking at her. Instead, the mayor and the woman whose daughter had been offered as the initial sacrifice had tight grips on Ellen's arms.

'No. Leave her alone.' Merry fought to get through the people blocking her in.

Mayor Crighton met her eyes over their heads. 'It's the only way.'

'The golem will kill her. She's a healer. She helps people.'

His eyes slid away, even as his jaw clenched and he tugged Ellen closer to the edge of the chasm. Anger flared inside Merry and a gust of air burst out of her staff, knocking the people in front of her to the side. She ran towards Ellen as a streak of black caught her eye.

Sadie darted in from the side and tangled up the mayor's legs. He stumbled, and Ellen wrenched her arm from his grip, then she swung a hand and punched the woman on her other side in the stomach.

The woman let go, doubled over, and Ellen scrambled backward, away from the edge of the chasm. Relief surged through Merry, but they weren't safe yet. She swung her staff to hit the mayor on the back of his head as he turned to chase Ellen.

He swivelled to face Merry, rage in his expression as he lurched towards her. She darted out of his reach, but then came up against a wall of bodies. The villagers were crowded at her back, giving her no room to move. One reached out and grabbed hold of her staff, crying out in pain as he did so but still refusing to let go. Merry tried to wrench it out of his grip but others reached in to grab it as well and the staff was pulled out of her hands.

Then the mayor was in front of her. 'I was going to spare you. A mage from the Meadows' bloodline would be a powerful ally, with the guild set against us. But you leave me no choice.' With that he raised both hands and gave Merry a hard shove in the centre of her torso.

A scream was torn from Merry's throat as she fell backward, feet lifting from the ground, arms windmilling as she toppled over the edge of the chasm. She fell for an agonising second, staring up at the faces of the villagers as they leaned over the edge. Then a punishing clamp around her entire body brought her to a stop. The air in her lungs was forced out of her and she wheezed as they sought to refill. The punishing grip around her middle allowed no movement. She looked up and saw the gaping mouth of the golem heading straight for her. She was in its hand, about to be shoved into that mouth.

She screamed again and fought as hard as she could to get free, but it was like trying to move a ten-tonne boulder with her toe.

The mouth loomed even closer.

A flash of movement came from the sky behind the golem, then dozens more, and an eerie wail set up. Birds, hundreds of them, flew straight for the golem, flying through the wind that comprised its body with no apparent ill effect. More flew around its head, the sound of their wails deafening in the suddenly still air.

The golem batted at the birds with its other hand, the grip on Merry lessening enough that she could finally suck air into her lungs. Then a streak of silver appeared in the air in front of the golem's mouth, wings spread, facing Merry.

It was the bird from the inn, the one that had flown over her after she'd freed the one trapped in the magical cage.

It met her gaze and dipped its head, before giving its wings a mighty flap. A feather was dislodged in the movement and it floated down to Merry. She reached out and grabbed hold of it. The silver bird pivoted in the air and dived inside the golem.

The golem gave a roar and let go of Merry.

She screamed, feather clutched in her hand, eyes clamped shut, expecting to plunge to her death on the chasm floor.

But she didn't fall.

She opened her eyes and gaped at the silver nimbus that surrounded her. It came from the feather in her hand. She looked up to see the silver bird emerge from the golem's head and fly towards her. She experienced a tug from the feather in her hand and the nimbus shifted, following the bird's flight path and taking her with it.

Soon she stood back on the edge of the chasm, in front of the mayor who had just tried to sacrifice her, her staff on the ground near his feet. His mouth gaped open, but no words emerged as he looked from her to the silver bird.

Merry had no time to worry about him. She picked up her staff and twisted to look to where the birds were still flying around the golem. It was batting at them with its hands, roaring, fresh wind currents filling the air. Many of the birds avoided its flailing hands, but others were hit and tumbled through the sky. Merry gasped, sure the downed birds were dead. But the silver bird wove through the commotion, a bright nimbus flaring in the air around the birds who had been struck until they righted themselves and flew off.

Even with the silver bird's help, the other birds had to be tiring. Their dives grew shorter, until soon they had all backed off and hovered in the air out of the golem's reach. It still sought to get to them, and the wind that had been swirling in the chasm now rose to batter the birds. They retreated, with the wind chasing them. Soon only the silver bird remained, hovering in the air in front of the golem, the wind gusts having no apparent effect on it.

Eventually the golem stopped trying to reach the fleeing birds and turned to face the silver one. It roared, the gust of wind from its mouth pushing over many of those arrayed around Merry. She had one end of her staff firmly planted on the ground between her feet and, though the wind whipped at her hair and clothes, she wasn't pushed back like the others.

The silver bird leisurely flew away from the golem to hover in the air in front of Merry. A flash of lightning swept over its wings, and a similar flash came from the feather she still held, a shock running down the staff it was pressed against by her palm.

'A silver falcon. I thought they were extinct.' Ellen's voice was filled with wonder. 'It saved you. Why?'

'I freed a bird that was caged in the stables back at the inn. When I came out of the stable the silver bird appeared and it flew off with the bird I freed.'

'Master Gin's bird? The one he thought his son had let escape?'

'Yes.' Merry grimaced at the fresh surge of guilt that arose at letting the son wear the blame for her actions. 'The cage was too small, and the roof and sides were electrified. The poor bird was getting shocked any time it moved. I had to free it.'

Ellen gave a nod. 'I would have done the same. No creature deserves to be caged or abused.' Her gaze darkened as she surveyed the mayor and the others around them. 'Not even them.'

The spokesman cleared his throat, shame darkening his gaze. 'We had no choice.' He winced when the golem roared at the birds hovering in the air a safe distance away from it. 'We still have no choice. A silver falcon is a wondrous thing, and glad I am that it intervened, but it is not strong enough to defeat a wind golem. If we do not find an Air mage, a fully trained Air mage,' he said with an apologetic nod at Merry, 'we will have to go ahead with the sacrifice.'

Merry clutched Ellen's arm. 'You are not sacrificing her.'

'The healer will not be harmed.' He turned to look behind him, at the woman who had first suggested using Ellen or Merry as the sacrifice.

She shook her head, fresh tears filling her eyes and spilling down her cheeks. 'Not my Lindy. Please. Pick someone else.'

Mayor Crighton's voice was grave as he said, 'We have been over this before. She contributes least to our community. We cannot spare anyone else.'

'It's not her fault she's not right in the head. It was the sickness that weakened her body as well as her brain. You can't punish her for that.'

'Someone has to be sacrificed, Margaret.'

'Then take me. Not Lindy.'

'And who would care for her if you died? None of us wishes to be saddled with such a burden.'

Margaret scanned her fellow villagers, expression pleading, but none of them met her gaze. She crumpled, almost falling, but then she straightened, determination replacing the hopelessness in her face.

'I'll not let you kill my daughter.' She made to run to

the edge of the chasm, but the mayor caught her arm and wrestled her to the ground.

Tears pricked Merry's eyes at her panicked screams as two men pushed a young woman with tangled long blonde hair and unblinking eyes forward.

'No.' Merry stepped into their path, holding up her staff. 'You are not throwing her to the golem.'

Her staff glowed as she commanded a wind to rip the men holding Lindy away. Then she angled the wind to force the mayor to step back from the girl's mother.

The woman's anguished screams faded as she got to her feet and ran to her daughter's side, embracing her while throwing Merry a grateful look. The look turned to one of horror when the wind protecting them fizzled out.

Merry slumped over and would have fallen if not for the staff helping to prop her up.

The mayor stepped forward. 'You can't fight off all of us. The girl must be sacrificed, or you doom us all.'

Heavy gusts of winds pulled and pushed at Merry as the golem gave up on trying to get to the birds beyond its reach and returned its attention to the people standing near the edge of the chasm.

Mayor Crighton was right. She couldn't fight an entire town, let alone the golem. But she was not going to let them kill an innocent woman.

Somehow, she had to figure out how to do the impossible.

# CHAPTER 12

Mayor Crighton turned away from Merry and gave the order for more men to grab Lindy, and then ordered a second lot to stop the mother from interfering a second time. Margaret cursed loudly, punching and kicking out at anyone who got close as she fought to get through the press of people to protect her daughter. There were too many of them. They forced her back, and when Merry tried to move, to do something, she was also boxed in.

'You can't do this,' she called out after the mayor. 'It's not right. There has to be another way. Just give us the chance to find it.'

He didn't answer, but when shouts rose up in the back of the crowd and sounds of fighting could be heard, she hoped her plea had got through to some of them. Then a tall figure pushed through the crowd and stood in front of Mayor Crighton, a wave of wind easing his path and blowing back his blue and white robe, while a grey and white cat strode at his side.

Gabriel Fairweather.

At his back were Kassandra and the other enforcers. Kassandra was glaring at Merry and Ellen, but the others were looking over her head, to where the wind golem was looming out of the chasm. Merry glanced over her shoulder at it, surprised it wasn't attacking them with wind. It was standing still, though its body never ceased its swirling, and she could see the vortex in its head spinning faster and faster.

Then her attention was pulled away when Mayor Crighton lunged towards Gabriel.

'This is your doing.' He threw a punch, but Gabriel dodged it easily as one of the enforcers waved a clenched fist. The mayor grunted as he was frozen in place, muscles straining, face reddening as he fought to break free from the invisible bonds.

'It is against guild law to summon an elemental golem,' said Gabriel, his tone even, though his brow was furrowed as he glanced at the golem in question. He shifted his gaze to Merry for a moment and then looked back to the mayor.

'Release him,' said Gabriel, and the unseen force holding Mayor Crighton immobile was lifted.

Goose bumps rippled over Merry's skin. Someone was doing magic nearby. Gabriel was speaking to the mayor, so she didn't think it was him, while Ellen was at her side. She had never reacted to enforcer magic before so it couldn't be them. Still, she scanned them and saw they all had their attention fixed on Gabriel and the mayor, except for one man who was staring intently at the golem.

'How long has the golem been troubling your town?' Gabriel asked.

'Three days,' said Mayor Crighton, a bitter twist to his mouth. 'It appeared the day after one of your enforcers deemed our tithe to the guild to be insufficient. When we said we could not pay more, he called me a liar, and said I was trying to cheat the guild, and said our protection had been revoked.' He glared over Gabriel's shoulder, and pointed at the enforcer whose gaze was focused on the golem.

Then he looked to Gabriel again. 'You say it is against guild law to summon a golem, and yet the only people powerful enough to do so belong to the guild.'

Gabriel turned to the enforcer the mayor had indicated, but before he could do or say anything the golem gave a deafening roar and a blast of freezing air hit those on the clearing.

Villagers screamed and dropped to the ground, hands over their heads as the wind battered them. Even the enforcers were forced back, red robes whipping in the wind. The only two to remain standing were Gabriel and Merry. He shot her a startled glance, eyes widening as his gaze dropped to her staff. She looked down to see the silver feather was shining once more, and the silver nimbus had returned around her body. Sadie was huddled at her feet, the nimbus helping to protect her from the unrelenting wind, while Beethoven had leapt onto Gabriel's shoulder.

When the golem roared again, Gabriel flicked his gaze to the chasm. He raised his hands and a fresh wind swirled in the air, striking towards the golem. The goose bumps on Merry's skin increased as his wind whipped around the golem again and again, ripping away its substance with each lash. But the air that formed its body quickly reformed after each strike. Still Gabriel persisted, aiming his next strike at the head.

He was trying to get to the vortex.

Merry lifted her staff and pushed aside the weariness dragging at her body as she sought to add her wind to his, striving to break through the shield of air that formed in front of the golem. She hadn't been able to defeat the golem on her own, but maybe together she and Gabriel would be strong enough.

Then the golem switched tactics. No longer fighting their wind strikes, he reached out and grabbed hold of them, thrusting the wind into his body and doubling in size. This time, even with the protective nimbus from the silver feather, the wind buffeted at her. It wasn't working; the golem was absorbing whatever they threw at it and using it against them.

The next time the golem roared, Merry was pushed backward, colliding with Gabriel. He wrapped his arms around her, his chest at her back, helping to steady her. 'It's no use,' he said, head bent to shout in her ear. 'We're not strong enough to take it down. We need to find the person who summoned it. It's the only way to stop it without a sacrifice.'

Merry gave a nod, the wind whipping around them tossing her hair in front of her eyes. She clutched her staff and the feather. At her back, Gabriel stood firm against the gale the golem was throwing at them, and she had the sense he was pushing behind them with his own wind to keep them upright. But they couldn't remain this way forever.

From the corner of her eye she could see people being bowled over, screams erupting as they were battered by the wind. The temperature dropped and the goose bumps sweeping over Merry now had nothing to do with magic being used nearby. Her teeth chattered, the only warmth coming from where her back was pressed up against Gabriel. He tightened his arms around her, but his embrace did little to stave off the bitter chill of the golem's wind.

The enforcers fared little better, whatever magics they were able to employ no match for what was quickly becoming a deadly windstorm. The silver feather in her hand began to glow even brighter, becoming painfully hot in Merry's hand, but she didn't dare let it go. The protection it offered, added to whatever Gabriel was doing, was the only thing keeping them upright.

The golem's deathly cold roar finally come to an end and Merry could straighten up. Gabriel's arms loosened around her, but he did not let go. 'It's sucking in all the air around us. When he roars next, no one will be able to stand against it.'

The screams around them changed in pitch to become more frenzied as the truth of Gabriel's words was realised. The golem was sucking in the air, pulling the people with it. They tumbled over and over, heading for the edge of the chasm.

The feather pressed up against her staff pulsed and Merry gaped as an image appeared in her head, of her approaching the golem and stuffing it into the golem's mouth.

What the hell?

The image came again, so vivid and strong Merry gasped.

She tapped Gabriel on the arm. 'Let me go,' she said. 'I have an idea.'

For a long moment, he didn't respond, and then his arms fell away and she stepped clear of him, shifting her grip so she held the staff in one hand and the feather in the other. She felt the suction as the golem drew in the air around her, and it became harder to breathe, but she ignored her discomfort as she allowed the pull to speed her arrival at the edge of the chasm, leg muscles aching as she strove to remain standing.

She avoided looking over the edge as she drew closer, not wanting to contemplate the depths of the chasm and the ground far below, hardly able to believe what she was about to attempt.

'Merry, what are you doing? Come back. You'll be killed.'

She turned her head and saw Ellen clinging to Gabriel's arm, both of them leaning forward with the force of the suction from the golem's mouth.

'I know what I'm doing.'

At least she hoped she did. For all she knew, the vision, image, whatever it was, could have been sent by someone who wanted her to plunge to her death. But she had to try. People were clinging to anything they could find to stop themselves from being pulled over the edge of the chasm, but they were in a clearing devoid of trees, with only each other to cling to. To stop a sacrifice of hundreds of lives, she had to step off the edge.

With a deep breath, holding the feather up in front of her, Merry took the last step.

She dropped.

Ellen and Gabriel screamed her name.

Then the silver nimbus flared so brightly around her it was almost blinding. She clenched her eyes shut, dimly registering that the suction had stopped. All was silence.

Merry opened her eyes and saw the golem looming over her, impossibly large and malevolent. Its mouth opened even wider as one wind-swirled hand reached out to grab her. This time, with the silver nimbus around her, its grip was not punishing, but she was not any more comfortable as the golem pulled her towards its mouth. She drew close enough to feel the wind created by the vortex swirling in the centre of its head. She waited until she was so close that she could have reached out and touched the golem before releasing the feather.

It flew into the golem's mouth, making straight for the vortex and arrowing into its centre. A silver flash erupted, and the vortex stopped spinning. Then it started up again but going in the opposite direction, pulling parts of the golem into its core. Faster and faster it spun, the silver feather still inside it, as it continued to rip the golem apart.

The golem gave a roar that was substantially weaker than the ones that had come before, its empty free hand coming up to tear at its head, ripping huge swatches of air away as it fought to get to the vortex. The hand was sucked in, quickly followed by the arm. The golem shrank even as the vortex grew to immense proportions and Merry gave a cheer.

Then the hand that was holding her began to shake, the strands of air that comprised it arrowing towards the vortex. The golem was losing all structural integrity, and soon the hand holding her in place was almost gone. So was the silver nimbus that had protected Merry before.

A lurch came as the golem's hand was completely sucked into the vortex, leaving Merry hanging in the air above the chasm. She looked down at the rocky ground far below, relieved when she didn't immediately plunge to her death.

Then whatever had been holding her up vanished.

Merry had time to scream once, before a gust of wind spun her up and around and she shot over the edge of the chasm and tumbled into Gabriel's arms once more.

He fell backward, landing on the grassy clearing on his back with Merry lying on top of him. She peered into his light grey eyes.

He'd saved her.

His arms cradled her to his chest, his gaze never leaving hers, long strands of her hair falling down to create a curtain around their heads. She could feel the heat of his body, pressing into hers, their faces so close she caught a hint of minty breath.

Merry sucked in a breath as his hands pulled her even closer and heat flared throughout her entire body, a frisson of excitement. The way he stared at her. It was as if they were the only two people who existed.

Then someone coughed, and low groans set up around them as the people of Breezeway recovered from the golem's punishing effects. Merry flushed at the reminder she and Gabriel were far from alone and scrambled off him. As she got to her feet, she forced herself to also remember he was the enemy. He wanted to take her to the guild tower, where she would be made to bind her burgeoning powers to the guild and lose all hope of getting home and safeguarding the portal from witch hunters.

She straightened her rumpled dress, avoiding

Gabriel's eyes as she surveyed the people in the clearing. Many of them appeared dazed and sported bruises from the battering they had received, but at least they were alive. That was more than could be said for the golem.

She looked out over the chasm and saw the vortex was still spinning there, but it was much smaller than it had been when the golem had been absorbed into it. As she watched it grew smaller and smaller, its spin lessening, until soon there was nothing left in the air except for the silver feather.

As she watched, the silver feather floated through the air, coming towards her. Legs still shaky, she slowly walked to the edge of the chasm, lifting out a hand to pluck the feather from the air. Then she turned to face those on the clearing, not sure what was going to happen next.

Gabriel stood in the centre of the crowd, his enforcers at his back, all of them with their eyes focused on her. The enforcers wore expressions of disbelief or anger, but in Gabriel's gaze she saw admiration and something else. Concern. Like her, had he remembered they were on opposite sides?

He stepped towards her and Merry tensed, expecting him to try to arrest her again, but before he could say anything a roar of outrage came from Mayor Crighton.

'The guild will pay for this.'

Gabriel gave a jolt and broke eye contact with Merry, and then turned around to face Mayor Crighton, who was pointing at an enforcer who was sprawled on the ground, eyes closed, seemingly unconscious.

The mayor loomed over the fallen man and scowled at Gabriel. 'The backlash when the girl destroyed the golem knocked him out. He's the mage who summoned it.'

Gabriel shook his head. 'That's not possible. Karl is an enforcer, not an Air mage.'

Mayor Crighton's expression darkened and he raised clenched fists. 'He's the one who threatened us after we told him we couldn't pay double our usual tithe. I'm telling you, he's responsible for almost destroying our village. We nearly sacrificed one of our own because of him.'

Gabriel wore a troubled expression as he turned to Kassandra. 'Is it true? Is your brother an Air mage as well as an enforcer?'

Kassandra looked to Karl and then back to Gabriel, and for the first time since Merry had encountered her she was showing signs of hesitancy.

'Kassandra,' said Gabriel, frowning at her, no doubt also noticing her changed demeanour. 'Tell me the truth.'

'I'm not sure. He was always secretive about his abilities. But—' She stopped when an angry mutter arose from the townsfolk arrayed around them and eyed them nervously.

'But what, Kassandra?' Gabriel asked, drawing her attention back to him.

She dropped her gaze. 'As a child, he did show an aptitude for Air. I was surprised when he became an enforcer. He had always been stronger than me, but I assumed the guild had tested him and found this to suit him better.' She waved a hand at her red robes.

Gabriel went silent as he stared down at the unconscious man. Merry also stared at him, giving a start when she realised he was the one she had seen staring so intently at the golem before it had launched its last attack. That attack had cut off the mayor's accusations that he'd been responsible for the wind golem. It seemed Gabriel had come to the same conclusion as he heaved a sigh and turned to Mayor Crighton with a grim set to his features.

'I am sincerely sorry if you or any of the people of Breezeway have come to harm because of the actions of one of my men. He will be taken to the guild tower and questioned. If it is found that he was the mage who summoned the wind golem you can be assured he will be dealt with accordingly.' There was a hardness to Gabriel's voice, his stance suggesting he would see to the enforcer's punishment himself if necessary.

Mayor Crighton gave a bitter laugh. 'You really think he was not acting on guild orders? Ours is not the first town to run afoul of creatures such as the golem since the last increase in tithes was met with protest.'

Gabriel stiffened. 'You accuse the guild of treachery?'

'I do.'

Kassandra barrelled forward, chin jutting out, eyes

narrowed as she got between Gabriel and the mayor. 'It is you who is guilty of treachery. Trying to sow dissent against the guild. I hereby place you under—'

Gabriel grabbed her arm and pulled her back. 'Enough, Kassandra! We will determine the truth of this matter back at the tower.'

'You're going to let him get away with besmirching the honour of the guild?' Kassandra wrenched her arm from his grip. 'Your aunt will hear about this.'

He stared her down. 'Yes, just as she will hear about your brother's possible involvement in the summoning of an elemental golem.'

Kassandra blanched as Gabriel turned to face the other enforcers. 'Bind Karl so he is ready for transport.'

He waved away Kassandra's protests, and she stalked off after the others. Then Gabriel faced the mayor once more. 'You have my assurance I will get to the bottom of what happened here.'

Mayor Crighton narrowed his eyes. 'And if it turns out he was acting on guild orders? What will you do then, Master Fairweather?'

Gabriel's expression became pained, but his voice was steady when he said, 'Then I will bring the matter to the attention of the full guild. The guild was formed to protect the people, not punish or impoverish them. But I am sure that is not the case.'

The mayor snorted softly but said nothing more as he rounded up his people and led them away, leaving

Merry and Ellen alone on the edge of the chasm with Gabriel and the two cats.

Gabriel turned to look at Merry, his gaze troubled. But he gave a rueful smile as he gave a bow. 'I thank you for your assistance in defeating the golem.'

This time, it was Ellen who snorted. 'Assistance? Merry defeated it all by herself.'

Gabriel flushed. 'Yes, you are correct. Merry deserves the guild's thanks, for what she did. I am sure my aunt will be most pleased, when we reach the tower and I can tell her what you did, though even she may doubt the appearance of a silver falcon. They have been thought to be extinct for many decades.' He pointed at the feather she still held. 'That is an extremely valuable artefact. It will not do to display it so openly.'

Merry stuffed the feather in her bag, and then stiffened, something he'd said snagging in her mind. She shook her head. 'There is no "we". I am not going anywhere near the guild tower.' At least, she wasn't going there until she had the first four charms in hand.

Even then, it would be in secret. She was not getting caught up in the guild and whatever it was they were up to. She agreed with Mayor Crighton's suspicions, that the enforcer had to be acting on guild instructions. She also didn't like the idea of the doubling of their tithe. From what she had seen here and in Pillingston, the non-magical people were barely making a living as it was. To tax them even further bordered on criminal.

Gabriel pulled his shoulders back. 'After all you have

witnessed, I can understand why you would be hesitant to accompany me to the tower. But I must do my duty. As you have amply demonstrated here today, you are more than a simple healer. By guild law, all those with strong elemental abilities must present themselves to the guild for classification, training and assignment.' He held up a hand when Merry went to protest.

'As a stranger to our land, I realise you will not wish to join the guild, but I am honour bound to do my duty and take you there. I also vow to do what I can to convince my aunt that you are to be allowed to return to your own world, before the portal that brought you here is destroyed.'

Merry sighed. As always, he seemed to sincerely believe that his aunt would do the right thing. But then, he didn't know for sure who she was related to. Ellen had already announced the truth of her bloodline to the people of Breezeway. Gabriel would have his suspicions confirmed soon enough. Better he heard it from her.

'I'm sure you think your aunt would let me go. But I'm not. You see, my grandmother was Meredith Meadows, your aunt's sworn enemy.'

He paled when she mentioned her bloodline, but quickly rallied. 'My aunt will not penalise you for events that took place before your birth. She will see reason. It is your grandmother, after all, who has broken guild law. Just tell my aunt what you know about your grandmother and her whereabouts and she will let you go.'

'My grandmother is dead,' said Merry bluntly. 'And I

never met her when she was alive, so I have nothing to say to your aunt. I have to find a way home.'

She never got the chance to tell him about the need to return to Belwich to renew the wards on the portal. His eyes rolled back in his head and he slumped, falling to the ground in a heap.

Ellen stepped forward, with a grimace. 'The rate I've been putting their people to sleep, I'm not going to be popular with the guild.'

Merry looked at the sleeping mage. The lines of his face were clear now.

'He would never have let you go,' said Ellen with a sigh. 'He might have wanted to, but Gabriel Fairweather is well known for his loyalty to his aunt and the guild.'

*The healer is correct. Gabriel is loyal to a fault. I suggest you leave the area before any of his enforcers come looking for him.*

Merry looked to where Gabriel's familiar stood beside Sadie. Beethoven's green eyes glittered as he inclined his head, and then he pointedly turned his back on her.

*You heard the cat. Let's go.* Sadie sauntered off and Merry and Ellen followed. With the enforcers closeted away with their unconscious prisoner, and the people of Breezeway focused on their own problems, there was no one to prevent them from leaving. They hurried across the bridge and ran down the road, the journey much easier now there was no wind golem stirring up a storm.

'We'll cut across here,' said Ellen, striding off the

road and into the fields to the left. A large stand of trees could be seen in the distance. 'Once we're in the forest, they won't be able to spot us.'

'We can't leave,' said Merry. 'I don't have the charm for the spell to send me home.'

Ellen shot her a bemused look. 'You have the most powerful Air charm there is, a feather from a silver falcon.'

'Oh,' said Merry, patting her bag. Relief that she hadn't failed in her first task swirled through her. Yet she still had four more charms to collect, and the last one, Spirit, would be the hardest charm of all, given the location of the focal point.

'You were amazing, by the way,' said Ellen. 'I thought you were going to plunge to your death when you stepped off the edge of the chasm. You defeated a wind golem, Merry. That's an incredible feat. With training, you could be the strongest mage Tirana has ever seen.'

Merry wasn't so sure about that. She very nearly had plunged to her death. She may have destroyed the golem, but Gabriel had saved her life afterwards. Had she even thanked him? She couldn't remember. Though she did remember the feeling of his arms around her as they'd fought the golem together, and the way he had cradled her against his chest when he'd pulled her to safety.

Had he woken from Ellen's magically induced sleep yet? He'd have to be upset when he did. This was the third time she'd escaped from him. He'd also have other troubles to deal with, if it was true that Kassandra's brother had been the one to summon the wind golem.

Those were not her problems, and she shouldn't hope for a chance to see Gabriel again to thank him properly for saving her life or let her mind linger on how handsome he was.

She was in enough trouble as it was.

Her focus had to be on getting home before she encountered any more problems.

She followed Ellen and Sadie across the field, welcoming the shade when they reached the trees, hoping things would go much more smoothly when it came time to get the next charm. But so far, nothing about being accidentally transported to Tirana had proved to be easy.

If her luck held true, there would be many more obstacles to overcome and dangers to face. Merry just had to hope she was up to the challenge of whatever lay ahead. No matter what, she would never give up on finding a way home.

ACKNOWLEDGMENTS

As always, there are many people who have helped me from the moment I first came up with the story idea to when this book was finally ready for readers to enjoy. Without them, there would be no book.

First, I have to thank my designer, Pixie Covers, for creating the set of covers that inspired the Merry Magic series. The original set was eventually redesigned to fit the story better, but if I hadn't fallen in love with them Merry, and Sadie, would not exist.

My alpha and beta readers, Sue-Ellen, Danni, Donna, Jennifer and Lana, all helped to fine tune the first draft into an actual story, while Sally Odgers' editing skills helped to make it shine. Without the assistance of these wonderful ladies my story would be poorer.

I need to thank my family and friends who continue to support me and don't fuss too much when I disappear into the writing cave for hours on end and daydream about imaginary worlds.

Last but not least, thank you to my readers for taking a chance on a new series. I hope you stick with Merry as she continues her journey to find out what true magic entails.

# ABOUT THE AUTHOR

Shelley Russell Nolan is an avid reader who began writing her own stories at sixteen. Her first completed manuscript featured brain eating aliens and a butt kicking teenage heroine. Since then she has spent her time creating fantasy worlds where death is only the beginning and even freaks can fall in love.

The first two books in her debut adult urban fantasy series, *Lost Reaper* and *Winged Reaper*, were published by Atlas Productions in 2016, with *Silver Reaper* published in 2017 to complete the series. 2018 saw the release of her *Arcane Awakenings Novella Series*, while Odyssey Books published the first book in a new post-apocalyptic series in 2019.

Born in New Zealand, moving to Australia with her family when she was seven, Shelley currently lives in Central Queensland, Australia, with her husband and two young children. They share their home with two wrecking ball kitties, a deformed budgerigar and two energetic pooches.

Shelley loves to hear from her readers so feel free to contact her on Facebook or leave a review on Goodreads or on her website - shelleyrussellnolan.com

www.ingramcontent.com/pod-product-compliance
Lightning Source LLC
Chambersburg PA
CBHW030425120726
47903CB00003B/821